# An Old Flame For Ava

Wanda Peters

Published by Wanda Peters, 2024.

AN OLD FLAME FOR AVA

**First edition. April 1, 2024.**



ISBN: 979-8224039364

Written by Wanda Peters.

# Also by Wanda Peters

10 Reasons You Should Cuckold Your Husband
Cruel Wife, Slave Husband
Embracing My Inner Bitch
Erotic Short Stories of Dominance and Submission
Cuckolded By A Stranger, An Erotic Novel
Cuckolded By His Boss
The Hot Wife Club
Cuckolded and Bound for Punishment
Cuckolded By My Best Friend
Cuckold's Anonymous
An Anniversary To Remember
My Wife's Surprise
Training Her Cuckold Husband
A Little Devil in Georgia
His Mother's Advice
Addicted To High Heels or A Slave To My Wife's Boots
The Huntress
A Wedding to Remember
Evil Under a Western Sky
Cuckolding The Bootlicker
Bondage and Discipline 101
Tales of Love, Romance and Marriage
The Evil Therapist Returns
Cracks in the Vow Six Stories of Love's Demise
Two Books Of Domination And Legal Thrillers

An Old Flame For Ava

# Table of Contents

# An Old Flame For Ava

# Chapter One - Introduction

Ava Myers swept through the living room, her confident stride betraying nothing of the inner turmoil that had taken root in her heart. The way she carried herself, with that quiet confidence and an air of command, could make heads turn even in the most crowded of spaces. Her emerald green eyes, sharp and piercing, scanned the room with a practiced ease, lingering on the figure of Ethan, who sat comfortably in his favorite armchair.

His smile was warm, the kind of smile that could melt away the worries of a lesser woman. It reached his expressive brown eyes, which held a kindness so genuine it often disarmed those lucky enough to be on the receiving end. Ethan rose as Ava approached, standing slightly shorter than her statuesque frame but no less confident. He pulled her into his embrace, a gesture meant to convey the depth of his affection.

"Hey, beautiful," he murmured, planting a soft kiss on her forehead.

"Hey," Ava replied, her voice even, her face adorned with a practiced smile that matched his own. Yet, beneath that serene exterior, there brewed a storm of discontent.

For five years, Ava had been trying to stifle the burgeoning dissatisfaction in her marriage to Ethan. Even during their most intimate moments, when she should have felt the closest to him, she couldn't shake off the feeling that something essential was missing from their union—passion. The passion that once set their world on fire seemed to have dwindled to a smoldering ember, leaving Ava yearning for a heat she no longer felt.

As Ethan chatted about his day, his words washing over her like a gentle but forgettable breeze, Ava's mind drifted. She thought back to the early days when every touch sparked excitement, every kiss promised discovery. But now, their routines felt more like well-rehearsed performances than expressions of desire. Even now, as his hand lingered on her waist, it felt perfunctory, lacking the electricity that once jolted her to life.

She nodded along to his stories, forming responses that sounded engaged while her thoughts roamed unchecked. Inside, Ava grappled with guilt; she loved Ethan, truly, but love alone wasn't filling the void that craved something more, something wild and uncontained. She longed for a connection that transcended the complacency of comfortable love—a connection that consumed her, body and soul.

"Is everything okay?" Ethan's voice broke through her reverie, laced with concern.

"Of course," Ava said too quickly, her smile faltering just a fraction before she caught herself. "Just thinking about what to make for dinner."

She excused herself under the pretense of checking the kitchen, leaving Ethan with his easy smile that seemed increasingly foreign to her. Alone, Ava leaned against the cool granite of the countertop, allowing herself a moment of vulnerability. The reflection staring back at her from the polished surface bore the weight of her silent confession: she craved more than this gentle, tepid love—they both deserved more. But the courage to voice these truths remained elusive, trapped behind the facade of the perfect wife in a seemingly perfect marriage.

Ava stepped out of the house, the door clicking softly behind her. The crisp morning air was a jolt to her senses, momentarily easing the tightness in her chest. She let out a long breath she hadn't realized she'd been holding, allowing the rhythm of her steps to ground her in the present as she headed toward the town's bustling center.

Her list of errands was a mundane litany that offered comfort in its predictability: pick up dry cleaning, stop by the post office, grab groceries. With each task crossed off, Ava felt a semblance of control that eluded her within the confines of her marriage. Here, on these familiar streets, she moved with purpose and efficiency, her tall frame weaving through the crowd like a vessel steadfast on its course.

As she rounded the corner to the organic market, Ava's thoughts were interrupted by a voice, warm and startlingly familiar. "Ava?"

She froze, not daring to trust the sudden thump of her heart. Slowly, she turned to face the man who had called her name, her eyes widening as they met a pair of deep-set ones that she had not seen in years but recognized instantly.

"James," she breathed, the name hanging between them like a ghost from another life.

"Wow, I can't believe it's you," he said, his surprise genuine as their gazes locked. A lopsided grin spread across his face, stirring something inside her she thought had long since settled into dormancy.

"Me neither," Ava replied, the words feeling inadequate for the swell of emotions that threatened to surface. How peculiar, she mused, to stumble upon an echo of her past amidst the banality of running errands.

The unexpectedness of their meeting sent ripples through Ava's carefully curated world, threatening the normalcy she clung to. Yet, as they stood there reconnecting through casual conversation, she couldn't help but feel the pull of a once-familiar orbit, drawing her back to memories best left undisturbed.

James stood before her, unchanged yet entirely different. Sunlight filtered through the market's awning, casting a golden hue upon his broad shoulders. Time had refined his features; his jaw was sharper, lined with the faint trace of stubble that Ava remembered as sandpaper against her skin. His chestnut hair once rebelliously tousled, now fell in a neat, controlled way that spoke of maturity. The rolled-up sleeves of his crisp white shirt revealed forearms etched with subtle veins—a testament to quiet strength.

He leaned slightly forward, an unconscious gesture that reduced the distance between them. His eyes, a piercing shade of blue, held a depth that seemed to reach into her, stirring memories of whispered secrets and shared laughter. Memories that tugged at the corners of Ava's lips, tempting them into a smile that mirrored his own.

"Still prefer the organic apples, I see," James commented, nodding towards the fruit in her hand.

Ava chuckled, the sound mingling with the market's ambient noise, a familiar melody amidst the chaos. "Some things never change," she replied, allowing the moment to swell with unspoken history—a tapestry woven from moments both sweet and bitter.

Their conversation danced around the mundane, tiptoeing along the edge of what was and what could have been. Each word exchanged pulsed with an undercurrent of nostalgia, each glance a silent acknowledgment of the chemistry that had once bound them together. It was an instant bridge back to the days of reckless abandon, of tangled sheets and even more entangled hearts.

In James' presence, the world around Ava narrowed, the chatter of shoppers and the clatter of carts fading into a distant hum. There was only James, with his easy smile and eyes who still knew how to read her every thought. Just like that, time-reversed, peeling away the layers of the years that had passed, leaving Ava standing in the remnants of her youth.

Ava twisted the wedding band around her finger, a motion she found herself doing more often these days. The gold band felt heavier than it used to like the symbol of her commitment had somehow grown in mass with the weight of her unspoken truths. Beside her, James reached for a bunch of grapes, his arm brushing against hers, sending a current of warmth through her body that pooled in places she tried to ignore.

"Remember our picnics at the park?" James asked, his voice low and teasing, laden with memories of sunlit afternoons and the taste of stolen wine on their lips.

A pang of longing struck her, sharp and unexpected. Ava's gaze flickered to his hand momentarily resting near hers, the hands that once explored every inch of her skin, igniting fires that had since been reduced to embers. She swallowed hard, the sound lost in the hustle of the market.

"Those were different times," Ava managed to say, her voice steady despite the chaos raging within her. She thought of Ethan, with his gentle eyes and endearing smile, the man who had promised to love her in sickness and in health. Guilt gnawed at her insides; she shouldn't be entertaining such thoughts, not when she belonged to someone else, not when she had vowed to be true.

But there was no denying the magnetic pull towards James, the way her heart seemed to recognize him as if he were a part of her it had been yearning for. In his presence, the dissatisfaction that lingered at the edge of her marriage crept closer, whispering seductive what-ifs into her ear.

"Time has a funny way of bringing people back into your life, doesn't it?" James mused, his gaze piercing hers with an intensity that spoke volumes.

"Sometimes I wonder..." Ava trailed off, the rest of her thoughts too treacherous to voice. Her fingers tightened on the apples in her basket, the crisp texture grounding her to the present. She couldn't afford to slip, not when the slope before her threatened to crumble beneath the weight of her reawakened desires.

"Life's short, Ava," James continued, oblivious to the war waging inside her. "We're not meant to live with regrets."

She nodded, more to herself than to him, a silent affirmation to stay the course. Yet, as she turned away from James to continue her errands, Ava couldn't shake the sensation of being watched, of leaving something precious behind. Her heart raced, caught between the safety of loyalty and the dangerous allure of a past love rekindled.

"Take care, James," she said without looking back, her voice carrying a finality that belied the uncertainty churning within her. With each step away, Ava felt both the relief of escape and the sorrow of departure, a dichotomy that left her restless and yearning as she vanished into the anonymity of the crowd.

Ava's fingers trailed along the smooth fabric of her coat, a motion meant to soothe the tempest brewing within her as she continued her errands. The unexpected encounter with James lingered in her mind like a stubborn perfume, infiltrating her senses with each step she took through the bustling aisles of the grocery store.

For years, Ava had been certain of her place in the world, confident in her role as Ethan's wife. Yet now, with James' lingering gaze imprinted on her memory, a longing she thought had long since faded began to unfurl within her. It was a yearning not just for the touch of a past lover, but for the woman she once was—wild, untethered, and unafraid of the depths of her passion.

"Focus," she whispered to herself, selecting a carton of eggs with more care than necessary. The simple act of shopping became her anchor, a lifeline thrown into the tumultuous sea of her thoughts. Each item she placed in her cart was a silent testament to the life she had built—a life full of stability, love, and promises spoken in the soft light of dawn.

But promises were ethereal, and as Ava passed by the floral section, the scent of roses hit her, sharp and sweet—the same fragrance she used to wear when she was with James. Her heart clenched, betraying her composure. The ache for that lost part of herself grew stronger, and she could almost feel James' hands tracing the contours of her body, reigniting a fire she thought had been extinguished beneath the comfortable companionship of her marriage.

"Stop it," she chastised herself, squeezing her eyes shut for a moment as if to banish the vivid images from her mind. She needed to remember the countless mornings waking up to Ethan's tender kisses, the gentle way he'd brush the hair from her face, the steady heartbeat against her ear as they lay entwined.

"Can I help you find anything?" a store employee's voice cut through her reverie, and she forced a smile.

"No, thank you," Ava replied, her voice steadier than she felt. "I'm almost done here."

Leaving the store, Ava welcomed the cool air on her flushed cheeks. Her fingers clutched the grocery bags like a shield, each step away from the store a deliberate march toward the life she had chosen. The sense of duty, the commitment to Ethan—it all wrapped around her like a second skin, one she feared might suffocate her if she dwelled too long on the what-ifs.

With every stride towards home, Ava wrestled with the resurgence of her desires, each one an insidious whisper questioning her resolve. But she would not falter; she couldn't. For in the quiet sanctuary of her heart, where fantasies dared to tread, Ava knew the true cost of surrendering to temptation. It was a price she wasn't willing to pay—not yet, anyway.

Ava's fingers trembled as she inserted the key into the lock, her other hand still gripping the grocery bags with a ferocity that belied her inner turmoil. The familiar click of the latch brought no relief to the tightness in her chest, only a reminder of the façade she had maintained for so long.

"Back already?" Ethan's voice, warm and tinged with surprise, floated from the living room.

"Traffic was light," Ava called back, her tone carefully neutral as she stepped inside their shared home, a place that suddenly seemed more like a beautifully gilded cage.

She set the bags down with more care than necessary, her movements deliberate, each one a silent declaration of normalcy. As she unpacked the groceries, the coolness of the refrigerator's interior felt like a balm against her heated skin, a momentary escape from the heat that James' unexpected presence had ignited within her.

"Everything okay?" Ethan asked, emerging into the kitchen with concern etched on his kind face.

"Fine," Ava replied, the word a half-truth that lodged itself in her throat. "Just tired is all." She forced a smile, but it didn't quite reach her eyes—the same eyes that had locked with James' not an hour before.

"Let me help you with that," Ethan offered, reaching for the milk carton just as Ava's hand closed around it. Their fingers brushed, a simple touch loaded with years of companionship and shared history. Yet, Ava couldn't help but compare it to the electric jolt she'd experienced at the mere sight of James.

"Thanks, I've got it," she said quickly, pulling back. Her heart clenched at the fleeting hurt that flashed across Ethan's face.

"Okay. I'll just... set the table then," he said, retreating, leaving Ava alone with the cacophony of her thoughts.

As she stored the last of the groceries, her mind raced, images of James interspersed with scenes of domestic tranquility with Ethan. Love and desire warring within her, pulling her apart at the seams. She needed time, space to think, to breathe.

"I'm going for a walk," Ava announced abruptly, surprising even herself.

"Before dinner?" Concern laced Ethan's question as he watched her grab her coat.

"Need some fresh air," she said, avoiding his gaze. "Won't be long."

"Alright," Ethan replied, resigned. "Be safe."

The door closed behind her with a soft click, and Ava was alone in the twilight. The air was crisp, carrying the promise of night's approach. She walked aimlessly, her steps echoing the chaos of her heart—a rhythm without melody, a dance without steps.

Her marriage, once a source of pride and joy, now felt like an anchor, dragging her deeper into waters too turbulent to navigate. The thought of James, with his undeniable charisma and the memories they shared, tempted her like a siren's call.

And yet, as she paused at the corner of their quiet street, bathed in the glow of the setting sun, Ava knew the gravity of her next choice would ripple through the fabric of her life. She stood there, silhouetted against the dying light, torn between the comfort of the past and the unknown whispers of a future that might never be.

# Chapter Two - Exploration

Ava slid into the velvet embrace of the café's secluded booth, the shadows playing across her face as she settled across from Sophia. The low thrum of ambient jazz mingled with the distant clink of china, wrapping the space in a cocoon of privacy. She leaned forward, forearms resting on the mahogany table, her emerald eyes flickering like twin beacons in the dim light.

"Thanks for meeting me here," Ava whispered, her voice carrying the weight of unspoken secrets. The soft glow of the candle between them danced across her features, highlighting the subtle contours of anxiety etched along her normally composed visage.

Sophia offered a reassuring smile, her presence a silent anchor in the sea of Ava's turmoil. "Of course, Ava. You know you can tell me anything."

For five years, Ava had been trying to stifle the growing void within her marriage to Ethan. It was like a silent scream trapped beneath the surface of her skin, desperate for release, yet stifled by the confines of her commitment. Even during their most tender moments, she couldn't help but feel a disconnect, an absence of fulfillment that left her craving more.

She took a deep breath, her full lips parting slightly as she exhaled the truth that had been simmering within. "Ethan is wonderful, and I love him, I do... but," Ava paused, her fingers tracing the rim of her coffee cup, "something is missing. In our bed, in our connection. It's like we're speaking different languages when it comes to desire."

There was no judgment in Sophia's gaze, only understanding. With every confession, Ava felt the layers of pretense peeling away, revealing the raw yearning that had been lurking in the depths of her heart. She wanted passion, the kind that consumed and ignited, leaving nothing but ashes and the promise of rebirth in its wake.

"I long for...more," Ava continued, her voice barely above a murmur, as though saying it louder might make it too real, too dangerous. "I need to be touched, explored, consumed in ways Ethan doesn't seem to understand. Or maybe he's just incapable of it." Her fingers tangled in her raven-colored hair, a gesture of frustration and longing.

"Sexual fulfillment is important, Ava," Sophia said softly, her words threading through the intimate space. "You deserve to have your needs met, to feel that fire and intensity."

Ava nodded, her eyes reflecting the flicker of hope that Sophia's words ignited. It was a validation she didn't realize she'd been seeking until now.

"Thank you, Sophia," Ava breathed out, the words heavy with relief and burgeoning determination. She knew what she needed to do, even if the path before her was shrouded in uncertainty. Tonight, she acknowledged the hunger within, a hunger for a connection that set her soul ablaze, a hunger for something, or someone, who could speak the language of her desires without translation.

Ava's hand wrapped around the warmth of her coffee mug, seeking comfort that the ceramic surface couldn't provide. Across from her, Sophia's gaze held steady, an anchor in the storm of Ava's confessions. The café buzzed with hushed conversations and the occasional clink of spoons against porcelain, but at their table, a sacred silence had settled.

"Thank you for listening," Ava whispered, her emerald eyes swimming with unshed tears. "It feels like I've been locked away from myself, and now...now I'm just trying to find a way back."

"Finding yourself is a journey worth taking," Sophia replied, her voice low and soothing. "You're not alone in this, Ava. I'm right here with you."

The reassurance in Sophia's tone unraveled something tight in Ava's chest, loosening the knots of her resolve. She glanced down, tracing the rim of her cup with a delicate finger, buying time before she dared to venture into deeper waters.

"There's more," Ava said, pausing as if testing the weight of her confession. She lifted her gaze, locking onto Sophia with a vulnerable intensity. "I saw James last week—completely by accident. It was just for a moment, but it felt like being struck by lightning."

"James?" Sophia leaned in, her brow furrowed, a silent invitation to continue.

"The memories came flooding back—the way he knew exactly how to touch me, to send shivers down my spine. We were volatile together, unpredictable." Ava's voice grew distant, lost in the labyrinth of the past. "He always left me breathless, craving more."

"Sounds intense," Sophia murmured, her eyes never leaving Ava's face.

"Intense doesn't begin to cover it," Ava confessed, a tremor in her voice. "He was the kind of lover who made you forget your name, who could read your body like poetry." She looked away, cheeks flushed with the raw honesty of her revelation.

"Seeing him again stirred something inside me," Ava continued, her pulse quickening at the admission. "Something I thought was long buried. I can't help but wonder...what if?"

Sophia reached across the table, her touch light on Ava's hand—a gesture of solidarity. "What ifs are powerful things," she acknowledged. "They can haunt us or they can free us. Only you can decide which path they lead you down."

Ava nodded, feeling the gravity of her words. Her heart was a wild thing within her chest, beating a rhythm laced with longing and the ghost of touches from a love long lost.

Ava's fingers curled around the warmth of her coffee cup, the porcelain a contrast to the tempest brewing within her. Sophia's gaze was unwavering, her presence a calm anchor in the storm of Ava's confession.

"Life is too short for what ifs," Sophia said gently yet firmly, leaning back against the wooden chair that seemed to absorb the soft hum of the café. "If James has reawakened something in you, something essential, don't you owe it to yourself to explore it?"

The words hung between them, powerful and charged as the air before a storm. Ava felt the weight of possibility press upon her chest. Could she truly consider stepping out of the bounds of her marriage, even if her heart yearned for the kind of passion that had once set her world ablaze?

"Explore it?" Ava repeated, her voice barely above a whisper, as though the very act of speaking could shatter the fragile veneer of her life.

Sophia nodded, her expression one of understanding and conviction. "Yes. To rediscover what makes Ava Myers come alive. You're not just Ethan's wife; you're a woman with desires, dreams, and an appetite for passion. You deserve fulfillment, Ava."

Ava's eyes widened, the green irises reflecting the flickering candle on their table. Excitement fluttered in her stomach, a sensation she hadn't felt in years, mingling with a trepidation that tethered her to reality. Her heart beat faster, acknowledging the truth in Sophia's words. She had a choice to make, a path to choose.

Could she dare to walk down the road not taken, to embrace the fire that James had once ignited within her? The thought sent a shiver through her body, her mind teetering on the precipice of decision. Ava realized then, with a clarity that cut through doubt, that her next move could redefine the very essence of her being.

Ava inhaled deeply, her breath catching on a mixture of determination and trepidation. The café's dim lighting cast shadows over the uncertainty etched into her features but also seemed to spotlight a newfound resolution in her gaze. With Sophia's words still echoing in her mind like a siren's call, Ava made her choice. She would seek out James; she would rekindle what had once been an inferno of passion between them. The thought sent a thrill coursing through her veins, quickening her pulse with the promise of what could be.

"Thank you," she whispered to Sophia, the words laden with gratitude and the weight of a decision that could alter her life's trajectory. Sophia merely offered a supportive smile, a silent ally in the pursuit of Ava's happiness.

Later, alone in the sanctuary of her bedroom, Ava found herself ensconced in the soft glow of her bedside lamp. Ethan was working late again, the house silent save for the occasional distant bark of a neighborhood dog. Her fingers trembled slightly as they caressed the spine of an unassuming book, its pages filled with stories of desire, exploration, and uninhibited yearning.

As she flipped through the erotica, each tale unfurled before her eyes like the petals of a night-blooming flower, revealing hidden depths and carnal secrets that resonated within her core. These were not just stories; they were reflections of her own suppressed cravings, of the sensual woman who had been lying dormant beneath layers of routine and dissatisfaction.

With each word she read, Ava felt herself drawn deeper into the realm of fantasy, where longing was met with fulfillment, and whispers of touch became symphonies of ecstasy. Here, in the privacy of these pages, she allowed herself to imagine James' hands upon her once more, skilled and knowing, reigniting the spark that had never truly extinguished.

Her heart raced as she envisioned their reunion, the way their bodies might entwine with a hunger that had only grown with time. Ava's skin tingled at the thought of his lips tracing familiar yet forgotten paths, awakening every nerve ending with deliberate intent.

It was this sensory immersion, this indulgence in the erotic tales that stoked the fires of her anticipation. No longer could she deny the stirring of her flesh, the deep-seated ache for connection, and the taste of forbidden fruit that dangled so temptingly before her.

And so, with the courage summoned from the daring escapades of the characters on the page, Ava reached for her phone. Her fingers danced hesitantly over the keys, composing a message to James that was both an invitation and a revelation of her desires.

"Let's meet," she typed, her heart hammering against her ribs as she poised her thumb over the 'send' button. With a breath that felt like the first gasp of air after emerging from underwater, Ava pressed down, sealing her fate and igniting the flame of possibility.

Ava turned another page, the paper's whisper a sharp contrast to the thundering of her heart. The narrative before her spoke of longing and reunion, of lovers entwined in rediscovery, their passion a force that defied time and circumstance. Each word resonated with Ava, echoing her hidden yearnings, and amplifying the memories she harbored of James.

With each scene that unfolds in the book, Ava's mind painted over its canvas with hues drawn from her palette of experiences. The characters' fiery encounters blurred into flashes of her past with James—the way his gaze seemed to peel away her layers, leaving her feeling vulnerable yet fiercely alive. It was as if the author had reached into the depths of her soul, plucking out the secrets she kept locked away, and spilling them onto the pages for her alone.

Her breath caught as she absorbed a particularly vivid passage, one where the protagonist surrendered to the touch of her long-lost love, a touch that whispered promises and teased dormant desire back to life. Ava felt the heat bloom in her cheeks and spread through her veins, a warmth that pooled in her core and throbbed with an urgency that startled her.

She closed her eyes, allowing the fantasy to consume her, to fill the void that had grown within her marriage. In her mind's eye, she saw James—the intensity of his stare, the curve of his smile that knew too much. She imagined him closing the distance between them, his hands reaching out to cradle her face, thumbs brushing her lips as if he could still taste her.

The possibilities of their next encounter sent her pulse into a frenzy, her body responding with a primal recognition. What would it be like to feel his skin against hers again? Would he still know how to draw out her pleasure, layer by layer, until she was nothing but a quivering mass of sensation?

Opening her eyes, Ava stared at the silent phone beside the book. The power to summon those possibilities into reality lay beneath her fingertips—a simple message, a few taps away from opening the door to the past they shared. But it was more than just a past; it was the potential of what could be, a future where her desires didn't have to hide in the shadows of her consciousness.

As the stories had fueled her courage, so too did they anchor her resolve. Ava no longer wanted to be a passive character in her tale of discontent; she craved to be the heroine who seized her happiness, who dared to reach out and grasp the ecstasy that beckoned. Her heart, once caged by fear and uncertainty, now beat with the rhythm of a woman awakened, ready to chart the course of her destiny—one that promised to be as tumultuous and as thrilling as the erotica that set her on this path.

Ava's hand hovered over the sleek surface of her phone, a tangible hesitation in the air before she commanded her trembling fingertips to make contact. She drew in a deep breath, steadying herself against the torrent of emotions that threatened to overwhelm her senses. It was now or never; this was the moment where she could either retreat into the safety of the life she knew or take the plunge into the depths of what she yearned for, with James as her beacon.

With each tap, her pulse quickened, a staccato rhythm in her veins that matched the cadence of her typing. The words on the screen were a confession, an invitation—a leap towards the fulfillment that had long eluded her within the confines of her marriage to Ethan. "James," she started, the name alone sparking a current that ran through her body,

"I've been thinking about us, about the fire we had. Can we meet? I want to explore... everything again."

The message was a raw exposure of her deepest wishes, stripped of pretenses and laid bare. A potent mix of trepidation and desire surged within Ava as she read it once more, her emerald eyes darting across the glowing pixels as if they held the key to unlocking the passion she so desperately craved.

Her thumb hovered over the 'send' button—its presence was a gateway to all the possibilities that danced at the edge of her consciousness. With a decisive press, the word transformed into action, sending her bold declaration across the digital divide toward James.

In the seconds that followed, time seemed malleable, stretching out infinitely as her heart pounded a fierce tattoo against her chest. Ava sat motionless, save for the rise and fall of her chest, her raven hair spilling over her shoulders like a dark waterfall, framing the anticipation etched on her face.

The silence of the room felt deafening, each passing second amplifying the weight of her decision. She knew the ramifications of this single message would ripple through the foundations of her marriage, potentially shattering the illusion of contentment she had carefully constructed over the years. But there was no turning back—the die was cast, and Ava was ready to face whatever storm it conjured, for her happiness was now the compass by which she navigated her life's journey.

The phone remained silent, an inert participant in the drama unfolding, yet its stillness belied the chaos of emotions swirling within Ava. She willed it to ring, to vibrate, to show some sign of life that would confirm her message had not gone unnoticed.

And then, with a suddenness that stole the breath from her lungs, the device came alive, its screen illuminating with an incoming response. Ava's future once shrouded in the haze of uncertainty, was about to come into sharp focus.

# Chapter Three – Ava's Dilemma

Ava's fingers hovered above her desk, a tremor betraying the turmoil within as she traced the outline of the glossy photograph before her. The image—a snapshot of joy with Ethan beaming beside her, his kind brown eyes filled with love—mocked her current despair. Her emerald gaze lingered on their clasped hands, bound by promises; now those vows felt like chains around her heart. With every breath, Ava fought the tide of memories, seeking the strength to uphold the resolution that churned in the pit of her stomach.

The room was silent except for the soft ticking of the clock, marking each second that brought her closer to irrevocable change. She inhaled deeply, her chest rising and falling with measured control, a testament to the inner steel that had carried her through countless challenges—a resolve that would not falter even now. The decision lay heavy on her shoulders, an invisible mantle that only she could feel.

Her hand reached out, almost of its own accord, and seized the sleek phone from its rest. Cool metal pressed against the warmth of her palm as she keyed in James' number, the digits etched into her mind through a haze of forbidden encounters and whispered confessions. Ava's pulse raced, a stark contrast to the stillness of her office. The familiar weight of longing and desire coiled within her, urging her forward, even as the specter of guilt gnawed at the edges of her resolve.

She paused, thumb hovering over the call button, her breath caught in her throat. This single action would sever the ties to one life and entwine her fate with another. Eyes closed, Ava summoned the image of James—the intensity of his gaze, the electric touch of his skin against hers, the way he stoked the fires of her passion until she was consumed by flames of ecstasy. Her body ached for the release she found only in his embrace, for the connection that transcended physicality and touched her very soul.

With a quiet exhale, Ava pressed down, sealing her choice with the click of a button. The phone buzzed against her ear, a lifeline cast into the unknown waters of her future. Each ring echoed the pounding of her heart, a drumbeat heralding the new chapter she was about to write—one where she allowed herself to explore the depths of her desires, unfettered by the confines of a marriage that had left her yearning for more.

Ava Myers was ready to claim her happiness, no matter the cost.

"Hello?" The word was a soft caress in her ear, the voice unmistakably James', wrapping around her like a warm embrace.

"James," Ava whispered, her voice unsteady, betraying the tumultuous storm of emotions brewing within her. "I... I've made my decision."

There was a pause, a moment stretched to infinity as she waited for his reaction, the silence between them charged with expectation.

"Tell me," he urged gently.

Ava's heart hammered against her ribcage, each beat a reminder of the path she was about to tread. "I want to be with you," she confessed, her words a mix of fear and longing. "I accept your proposal."

The line crackled with life as James absorbed her confession, and then, an exhalation of pure joy spilled from him into the phone. "Oh, Ava," he breathed out, the sound of his happiness weaving through the fibers of her being, igniting a spark that threatened to blaze uncontrollably.

"Are you sure?" James' voice was laced with disbelief, as though he had prepared himself for any answer but this one.

"More than anything," Ava affirmed, the certainty in her voice surprising even herself. She could almost feel James' smile through the miles that separated them, could envision the light in his eyes that had always drawn her in like a moth to flame.

"God, Ava... I—"

"James," she interjected, cutting off his elation, "we need to be careful. There are things I need to do here first." Her mind flickered to Ethan, to the conversation that awaited her, a confrontation that would inevitably shatter the calm surface of their shared existence.

"Of course," James responded, the undercurrent of his excitement still palpable. "We'll take it one step at a time."

Closing her eyes, Ava hung up the phone, the click of the call ending resonating like the final note of a somber melody. The room felt suddenly too large, too empty as if it were void of all the warmth that had just filled her ears.

She sat there, cradling the silent phone in her hands, the dichotomy of her emotions warring within her chest. Elation coursed through her veins, the prospect of being with James, truly with him, sent a thrill racing down her spine. Yet, entwined with that thrill was the sharp pang of guilt, the knowledge that her next words would irrevocably wound the man she had once vowed to cherish.

Ava stood, her movements robotic as she contemplated the impending confrontation with Ethan. She knew the hurt she was about to inflict, the look of betrayal that would soon cloud his kind brown eyes. It was necessary, she reminded herself—a bittersweet release from a union that had long since lost its fire.

Her fingertips traced the cool metal of the wedding band encircling her finger, a symbol of promises made and now broken. With a steadying breath, Ava readied herself for the fallout, preparing to dismantle the life she had built in pursuit of the passion that burned only with James. The weight of her decision hung heavy on her shoulders as she turned towards the door, stepping forward into an uncertain future.

Ava's heels clicked against the hardwood floor, a staccato rhythm that matched her racing heart. The living room lay before her, bathed in the soft glow of the evening sun filtering through half-drawn curtains.

Ethan was there, nestled in his favorite armchair, lost in the world of the novel cradled gently between his hands.

She paused at the entryway, watching him for a moment. There was a stillness about him, a contentment found in those quiet hours of reading that she had once loved to share. But now, as she stood on the precipice of change, that same stillness felt like a chasm between them.

Inhaling deeply, Ava stepped into the room, each breath an attempt to steady her resolve. She approached silently, then sat beside him, close enough to feel the warmth of his body yet miles apart in every way that mattered.

Ethan looked up from his book, his brown eyes searching hers—a silent question lingering in their depths. His smile faltered as he took in her solemn expression, the book slipping onto his lap, forgotten.

"Can we talk?" Ava's voice barely rose above a whisper, but it cut through the tranquility like a shard of glass.

There was a momentary hesitation, a furrowing of his brow before he nodded and closed the book, giving her his undivided attention. It was now or never.

"Eth—I've been feeling... lost," she began, her words faltering, betraying the turmoil within. "Our marriage hasn't been what I need. What I crave."

The air grew thick with unsaid words as Ethan's face transformed, the hurt and betrayal etching lines of confusion and pain across his features. Tears brimmed in his eyes, the kind eyes that had once been her harbor.

"And," she continued, her voice gaining strength even as her heart splintered, "I've made a decision. I'm going to be with James."

The name hung between them, a specter of the choices made in shadowed whispers and stolen moments. Ethan's hand twitched, a visceral reaction to the wound she had just inflicted.

"James?" His voice broke the single word a testament to the depth of his anguish.

Ava reached out, her fingers trembling as she sought to bridge the gap with a touch, an apology. But Ethan recoiled, pulling his hand away, leaving her grasp empty.

The space between them yawned wider, a gulf filled with the debris of a love that had once promised forever. And as the silence stretched, Ava knew that the echoes of her confession would haunt the hollows of the home they had built together, long after she walked away.

Ava watched a solitary tear navigate the landscape of Ethan's cheek, tracing a path of salted sorrow that mirrored her internal desolation. The silence that shrouded the room was deafening, punctuated only by the soft rustling of pages as Ethan's thumb ceased its absent-minded dance across the edge of his book. His brown eyes, once brimming with gentle warmth, now searched hers with a pained intensity.

"Tell me, Ava," he asked, his voice a fragile whisper threatening to shatter, "how long have you felt this emptiness? This... dissatisfaction?"

She hesitated, the words lodged in her throat like a boulder damming the flow of a river. It had been months—no, years—of pretending, of hiding behind half-smiles and silent pleas for something more, something deeper. Ava's pulse throbbed in her ears as she finally allowed the truth to surface.

"Too long," she admitted her voice barely above a breath, betraying the storm within. "I didn't want to cause you pain, Ethan. I thought I could overcome it, but..."

The unspoken words hung heavy between them: the yearning for passion left unfulfilled, the intimacy that never quite bridged their separate worlds. Ava's emerald eyes, usually so full of resolve, now shimmered with unshed tears of guilt and conflict.

Time became a meaningless concept as they sat there, enveloped in a cocoon of heartache. The room itself seemed to absorb the gravity of their fractured bond, the walls closing in with each silent second that ticked by. The world outside faded into oblivion, leaving only the crushing weight of reality pressing against them.

It was Ethan who broke the stillness, drawing in a deep breath that filled his lungs with the cold air of acceptance. His voice, when he spoke again, carried the quiet dignity of resignation.

"Ava," he said, the tenderness of his tone wrapping around her name like a final embrace, "I love you. I've always wanted nothing more than your happiness. If being with him... with James, is what you need, then I won't stand in your way."

There it was—the release, the permission she craved, yet it bound her heart in new chains of remorse. Ethan's selfless words were a testament to the love he bore her, a love that she once believed would be her anchor. Now, adrift in a sea of change, she clung to the remnants of a dream that had quietly died in the night.

"Thank you," she whispered, her voice a lifeline thrown into the void. But even as she spoke, Ava knew that gratitude was a paltry offering at the altar of their shared history—a history that was now closing its final chapter, leaving both of them to navigate the unwritten pages of tomorrow alone.

# Chapter Four - Confession

Ava paused at the threshold of the living room, her fingers lingering on the cool metal of the doorknob as she inhaled deeply. She could feel the weight of the impending conversation settle like lead in the pit of her stomach, each breath a silent mantra to brace herself for the revelations to come. Purposefully, she stepped into the space, her poise unwavering despite the inner turmoil that churned beneath her composed exterior.

Across the room, Ethan's presence was an anchor in the soft lamplight, his figure relaxed into the plush contours of the couch. His eyes, warm and tender, were lost behind the pages of a novel, yet the subtle shift in his brow betrayed a sensitivity to the unspoken words hanging heavy between them. It was that same keen perception that had once drawn Ava to him, a testament to the profound connection they shared beyond mere physical union.

As the silence stretched, Ethan marked his place with a gentle thumb and closed the book, setting it aside with quiet reverence. The tension that coiled in the air seemed to tug at his features, knitting his brow in a constellation of concern. His gaze lifted, finding Ava across the expanse of their shared life, etched into every piece of furniture, every framed memory upon the wall.

"Is everything alright?" he asked, the question simple yet laden with the weight of a thousand unspoken fears. His voice cut through the stillness, a lifeline cast into the unknown depths of Ava's internal sea.

She met his eyes, those pools of earnest inquiry, and felt the resolve within her harden. This was the moment of truth, the precipice upon which the future of their love balanced precariously. She knew that whatever lay ahead, it had to begin here, with honesty, with vulnerability, with the courage to speak the words that had long been imprisoned within her heart.

Ava crossed the room, each step deliberate, her heart a staccato rhythm against her ribs. She lowered herself onto the couch, mere inches from Ethan, who radiated both warmth and concern. Her hands, unsteady as autumn leaves quivering in a pre-storm breeze, clasped together in her lap. The words she needed to say swirled in her mind like leaves caught in a whirlwind, each one heavy with consequence.

She turned to him, her emerald eyes locking with his brown ones, a silent communication passing between them. Here was the man she had pledged her life to, whose laughter filled the corners of their home, whose kindness was the melody to which her heart had attuned itself. Yet, within her chest, a discordant note had been sounding, growing louder over the years until it could no longer be ignored.

"Ethan," Ava began, her voice a whisper that seemed to carry the weight of the world, "I need you to know that I love you deeply." Her fingers found his, gripping them as if they were the anchor in the chaos that threatened to engulf her. "You have been my rock, my solace, my joy."

She paused, her gaze never leaving his face, reading the emotions that played across his features like shadows cast by a flickering flame. Her next words came on a breath, fragile yet resolute. "But there's a part of me," she continued, a tremor in her voice betraying the fear of wounding him, "that has felt...lost. My decision to explore this...this path with James is not a reflection on you, or us."

Ava watched as understanding dawned in Ethan's eyes, a testament to the bond that had always allowed them to communicate beyond words. She breathed in the scent of him, the familiar mix of sandalwood and citrus that had so often been a balm to her soul. Now, it underscored the gravity of what she had just shared, the precipice upon which they now stood.

"Nothing about my feelings for you has diminished," she assured him, her voice steady despite the chaos raging inside her. "It's not about your worth as a partner—never think that. It's something within me, a yearning I can't seem to quell. And James..." Ava trailed off, her resolve faltering for a moment as she searched Ethan's face for any sign of the pain she feared inflicting.

Ethan remained silent, his gaze unwavering, allowing her the space to navigate the labyrinth of her confession. In his eyes, she found a well of strength, and it gave her the courage to continue, to lay bare the truths that had long remained hidden behind the facade of contentment.

"James has awakened something in me," she admitted softly, her words spilling out like secrets long-held. "Something I thought I could ignore, but it's become impossible to do so."

Ava held her breath, the air in the room thick with the enormity of her admission, waiting for Ethan's response, for the next step in a dance that had suddenly changed its rhythm.

Ethan's brow furrowed, a visible testament to the storm of confusion brewing within him. In the quiet of the living room, his book lay forgotten, a silent witness to the unfolding drama. Ava watched, her heart echoing the tumultuous beat she saw in his chest, the way his breath seemed to catch as he attempted to process her words.

"Sexually unfulfilled," Ava began again, her voice a mere whisper against the tension that hung between them. "It's been lingering for some time now, Ethan." She took a deep, steadying breath, feeling the weight of her confession pressing down upon her. "Our marriage... it's been missing a vital piece, a spark I thought would rekindle with time."

Ethan's hand twitched on the couch, a small but telling gesture of the turmoil inside him. He looked away for a moment, his eyes searching the room for something intangible before returning to Ava's earnest gaze.

"Meeting James again," Ava continued, her voice gaining strength as she spoke her truth, "it was like being jolted awake from a dream I didn't realize I was having. He stirred desires in me, longings I'd pushed aside, thinking they were just fleeting thoughts, not something substantial, not something real."

She paused, watching Ethan absorb her words, his expression a tapestry woven with threads of shock and contemplation. Her pulse raced a syncopated rhythm with the gravity of what she had just confessed. They sat together, two hearts entwined by love yet divided by unspoken truths, embarking on a journey into the unknown.

With hands clasped together as if to keep her world from unraveling, Ava inhaled sharply, the air feeling thick in her lungs. She had laid bare a truth she could no longer hold within the confines of her heart. Ethan, still grappling with her revelation, shifted uncomfortably, his body language an echo of the inner chaos Ava's words had incited.

"Why, Ava?" His voice, usually so sure and comforting, now wavered, a tremulous note that struck her deeply. "Why didn't you come to me? If something was wrong...if you were unhappy...?" His brown eyes searched hers, seeking answers in the green depths that often promised safety and love.

Ava felt the sting of tears threatening to spill over, her resolve wavering under the weight of his confusion and pain. She knew the hurt that clouded his handsome features was a reflection of the silent battles she had fought alone.

"I was afraid," she confessed, her voice barely above a whisper. The admission tasted bitter on her tongue, a stark contrast to the sweet affirmations they'd shared in quieter, happier times. "Afraid of how it might hurt you, how it might shake the very foundation of what we've built." She sighed, a sound heavy with the burden of unspoken fears. "I couldn't bear the thought of losing you, Ethan. But these desires, this part of me that remained untouched and unseen, grew louder with each passing day. I tried to silence it, for us, but it's become a force I can't ignore."

Ethan's gaze held her own, the warmth that usually resided there now tempered by the cool onset of realization. His fingers reached out tentatively as if he too feared the fragility of their connection at that moment. They touched skin against skin, a lifeline amidst the storm of emotions that threatened to engulf them both.

"Even in our closest moments," Ava continued, her hand trembling within his grasp, "there was always this whisper of discontent, a shadow that loomed over the passion we shared. I thought time would heal, that love would be enough to chase away the doubts. But meeting James...it was like a mirror being held up to my soul, showing me the parts that lay dormant, yearning to be awakened."

The room seemed to contract around them, the walls bearing witness to the raw honesty that spilled from Ava's lips. It was a moment suspended in time, a crossroads where the path they would choose could mend or irrevocably alter the tapestry of their marriage.

Ethan's chest heaved, a silent testament to the turmoil that churned within him. His eyes, usually so full of warmth and clarity, now flickered with the shadows of confusion and hurt. But instead of giving voice to the cacophony of betrayal and pain that might have risen from any other man in his place, he pressed his lips together—a dam holding back the flood.

"James," Ava began, her voice a mere whisper but laden with the weight of confession, "he...he made me an offer." Her emerald eyes, which had often served as windows to her indomitable spirit, now shimmered with trepidation. She held Ethan's gaze, willing him to understand the gravity of what she was about to divulge.

"An offer?" Ethan's voice was strained, barely above a murmur, as if he feared the power his own words could wield.

Ava nodded, the motion slow and deliberate. "He said he would only be part of my...our life if it was built on honesty. If we...if we explored these suppressed desires together. With you."

The silence that followed was palpable, an entity in itself that seemed to envelop them both. The air felt thick as Ethan processed the implications of Ava's revelation. He sat motionless save for the almost imperceptible rise and fall of his chest, his hands resting limply in his lap, a stark contrast to the resolve that once defined his every gesture.

In that space of stillness, Ava watched the man she loved grapple with a reality that threatened the very foundation of their union. Each second that ticked by stretched into infinity, every heartbeat a drum roll to an uncertain future. Yet, there was no outburst, no harsh words or accusations—only the profound struggle of a kind-hearted man wrestling with a concept so alien to their shared existence.

"Exploring together," he finally echoed, the words sounding foreign on his lips. And then, after a deep breath that seemed to carry the weight of all their years together, he leaned towards her. His brown eyes, once stormy with hurt, now bore a glimmer of something else—perhaps the dawning understanding of the complex landscape of human desire.

"Okay," he exhaled, the simple affirmation hanging between them like a fragile truce, a single syllable bearing the potential to either bridge the chasm that had opened up before them or to widen it beyond repair.

Ethan's gaze locked onto Ava, a storm of emotions giving way to a sudden calm as he witnessed her raw candor. Her emerald eyes, often so sure and commanding, now shimmered with the honesty of her confession. In the vulnerability of her admission, Ethan saw not a betrayal but a plea for understanding—a silent acknowledgment that their love was worth fighting for.

"James... wants us to explore together?" Ethan's voice was tentative at first as if testing the waters of this new reality. The surprise in his eyes was replaced by a quiet realization, an acceptance that Ava's desires were not an indictment of their love but a complex facet of her humanity.

Ava's hands, still trembling, found themselves enveloped by Ethan's. His grip was firm and resolute, the warmth of his palms offering a silent reassurance. "Ava," he said, his voice low, threaded with a determination that seemed to anchor them both amidst the uncertainty. "I love you. More than anything. And if this... if embracing something unconventional is what it takes, then I'm here. We're in this together."

Their fingers intertwined, a tangible symbol of their unity, as Ethan grappled with the magnitude of his own words. He knew the road ahead would be uncharted, perhaps perilous. Yet in the depths of Ava's eyes, he found the courage to face whatever came next, buoyed by the unshakeable foundation of their shared love.

Tears pooled in Ava's eyes, a crystalline testament to the swell of emotions churning within her. As she gazed into Ethan's earnest brown eyes—eyes that had witnessed her soul's most intimate contours—a tremor of relief shuddered through her body. Here was understanding, profound and unwavering, radiating from the man she had vowed to journey through life with.

"Thank you," she whispered, the words barely audible yet heavy with meaning. It was a gratitude that stemmed not just from his acceptance but from the realization that their love was resilient, capable of bending without breaking under the weight of their trials.

Ethan's arms enfolded her, sturdy and encompassing, drawing her into the shelter of his embrace. Their bodies melded together as if to physically manifest the emotional tapestry they were weaving—a tapestry of trust, of shared futures, of love redefined.

In the warmth of his hold, Ava surrendered to the promise of new beginnings. Each breath they shared seemed to stitch their hearts closer, fortifying them against the uncertainties that lay ahead. But there, in the silent language of touch, doubts dissipated, replaced by the quiet conviction that together, they were invincible.

Ava disentangled herself from Ethan's arms, the lingering warmth of his embrace still wrapping her like a protective cloak. She angled her body to face him, her posture straight yet open—a mirror to the earnest resolve in her emerald eyes. The gravity of their conversation had settled, leaving space for the logistics that needed tending.

"Okay," she began, her voice steady and imbued with purpose, "we should talk about how this is going to work."

Ethan nodded, his demeanor reflecting the seriousness of their discussion. He shifted on the couch, creating an atmosphere conducive to the dialogue they were about to embark upon. His brown eyes, usually so full of mirth, now bore the intensity of focus.

"Boundaries," he said firmly, the word hanging between them as a cornerstone of their new path. "We need clear lines that we both agree on."

"Absolutely," Ava affirmed. Her fingers traced idle patterns on the cushion beside her, grounding herself in the tactile sensation. "We can't let this... exploration jeopardize what we have. It has to add to it, not take away."

"Then let's start simple," Ethan suggested, reaching for her hand and intertwining their fingers—a tangible connection amid the abstracts they were navigating. "Transparency. We don't keep secrets. No matter how uncomfortable it might be, we communicate."

"Agreed." Ava squeezed his hand, the pressure a silent testament to her commitment. "And respect. Our feelings for each other, our marriage vows—they remain sacred."

"Of course." Ethan's voice was resolute. "What about James?"

"James understands that while he may be a part of my sexuality, he isn't a part of our marriage," Ava clarified, her words carefully chosen. "He's... an experience. One that I want you to be comfortable with, Ethan. Always comfortable."

"And if I'm not?" Ethan asked, the vulnerability of the question bared for her to see.

"Then we stop," Ava replied without hesitation. "We reassess. This isn't about necessity, Ethan; it's about us exploring together, growing together in ways we haven't before."

"Right." A small smile cracked Ethan's solemn expression. "Together."

They fell into a companionable silence, each lost in contemplation. The depth of their love had been tested, but here they were, constructing a bridge over uncharted waters with mutual respect and unwavering trust.

"Let's promise, no matter what happens," Ava said, breaking the quietude, "our love stays at the core. That's non-negotiable."

"Non-negotiable," Ethan echoed, the promise sealed in the firm resolve of his tone.

As the evening waned, they continued to weave the delicate framework of their agreement, each term and condition strengthening the lattice of their bond. By the time they rose from the couch, a blueprint for their future lay before them—unconventional, perhaps, but one they were determined to build upon the unshakeable foundation of their shared love.

# Chapter Five – Setting Boundaries

Ava paced the length of the living room, her every step deliberate and measured, like a dancer counting the beats in her head. The soft carpet muted the sound, but Ethan and James could feel the weight of her movements in the charged silence that filled the space. They both sat on the couch, each claiming an opposite end, an unoccupied cushion between them serving as a no-man's land in this quiet battleground of hearts.

"Thank you," Ava finally said, halting before the sofa, green eyes capturing Ethan's with a gaze so intense it seemed to echo through the stillness. "For being willing to even have this conversation."

Ethan's smile was fraught with complexity, his kind brown eyes reflecting a storm of emotion he was trying hard to navigate. He nodded, knowing words would be too clumsy for what he felt. Instead, he reached out, his fingers gently brushing against Ava's hand—his silent way of saying, 'I'm here. I'm with you.'

"James." Ava turned slightly, granting him the same piercing attention she had given her husband. James held her gaze with a steady calmness, his presence in the room like a steadfast anchor.

Ava took a deep breath, the air filling her lungs and lifting her chest. She was the picture of composure, but beneath the surface, currents of nervous anticipation swirled. "I need you both to understand that this... exploration doesn't change how I feel about us," she said, her voice a low thrum that resonated with sincerity. "My commitment to you, our marriage, it's unwavering, Ethan."

She swept a lock of raven hair behind her ear, a small gesture betraying her need for reassurance. Her full lips parted to reveal that subtle dimple, a glint of vulnerability amidst her confidence. Ethan reached out again, this time capturing her hand fully in his, grounding her.

"Exploring" was such a benign word for the seismic shift they were contemplating, Ethan thought, but if it made Ava happy—no, fulfilled—it was worth wading through the uncertainty. His thumb traced circles over Ava's skin, a tactile reminder of their connection. This unconventional arrangement might test them, but he hoped, more than anything, it would bring back the spark that once set their world alight.

James shifted slightly, leaning forward with his elbows resting on his knees. He exuded an air of certainty that seemed to fill the room, a stark contrast to the tempest of emotions churning within Ethan. The silence stretched taut between them, each second ticking like a heartbeat waiting to be acknowledged.

"Listen, Ethan," James began, his voice a blend of strength and understanding, "this isn't about me taking something from you. It's not about replacement." He paused, his gaze steady, "It's about Ava, about her needs... desires that are unmet."

Ethan's chest tightened as he processed James's words, the gravity of their meaning weighing heavily on him. He watched the man who had become an intricate part of their lives, a part of Ava's innermost yearnings. It was like peering into a mirror that reflected a version of himself he didn't recognize—one riddled with doubts and shadows of jealousy.

"Her happiness is what's important here," James continued, "and somehow, in this tangled mess of emotions and flesh, we've found ourselves bound by that common thread—our love for Ava."

The air around Ethan felt charged, a static energy that pricked at his skin. He wanted to speak, to articulate the maelstrom inside him that both pushed him away and pulled him closer to the precipice of this new reality. But words were elusive creatures, flitting just beyond his grasp.

"James," Ethan finally managed, his voice betraying the turmoil beneath his composed exterior, "I can't pretend I understand all of this or that it doesn't scare me. It does. More than anything, I fear losing her—to you, to this." His hand gestured vaguely, encompassing the vast unknown they were stepping into.

He glanced at Ava, seeking solace in the familiar yet enigmatic green of her eyes. "But if this is what she needs, to feel complete," Ethan continued, his resolve hardening like steel tempered by fire, "then I'm willing to try. For her. Because making her happy is all I've ever wanted, even if it means redefining what our happiness looks like."

In the quiet aftermath of his confession, a fragile hope lingered, its presence as tentative as the first rays of dawn creeping past the horizon. They sat there, three souls navigating the complexities of want and love, bound together by the singular desire to see Ava fulfilled.

James shifted on the plush cushions of the couch, his posture relaxed yet charged with an assertive energy that contrasted sharply with Ethan's tension. He cleared his throat, drawing their attention. "I have an idea," he said, locking eyes with Ethan in a gesture of respect. "Something that might help us navigate these waters. Ava, how do you feel about dancing?"

Ava's face lit up at the mention, her emerald eyes reflecting a spark of excitement. She had always found freedom in the rhythmic sway of dance, a liberation of the soul that mere words could never achieve.

"James thinks," he continued, leaning forward with his elbows resting on his knees, "that taking you out dancing could be a good way for all of us to find our footing in this...arrangement. It's public, it's social, and there are boundaries inherent in the act itself."

Ethan's brow furrowed as he processed the suggestion, his mind racing with images of Ava in the arms of another man. The thought was both unsettling and oddly stirring.

"Of course," James added smoothly, "I think Ethan should come along. Not just as a bystander, but as part of this. To see you in your element, Ava, and to understand the connection—physical, yes, but not replacing what you two have."

Ava turned her gaze towards Ethan, her expression open and searching. She reached out, placing a hand gently over his, a silent plea for his understanding and consent. She needed him to know that this wasn't a ploy or a step towards separation; rather, it was an exploration they dared together.

"Are you okay with that, Ethan?" she asked, her voice tinged with hope and an undercurrent of concern. Her thumb stroked the back of his hand, a tender gesture meant to bridge the chasm of doubt that threatened to swallow them whole.

Ethan's heart pounded against his chest, a cacophony of fear and love playing a discordant melody. But as he looked into Ava's eyes—those deep pools of green that had captivated him since the day they met—he found a resolve he didn't know he possessed.

"Okay," he exhaled, the word a testament to his commitment to her happiness. "Let's go dancing."

# Chapter Six – Heating Up

The heavy door of the bar swung open with a well-worn creak, and Ava Myers led the way inside, her purposeful stride carrying her into the heart of the local haunt. The rich twang of country music wrapped around them like a warm, familiar blanket, and Ava's emerald eyes sparkled with an excitement that had been absent for too long. She could feel every eye upon her as she moved, her raven-colored hair a stark contrast against the dimly lit backdrop.

Ethan trailed behind her with his usual easy grace, a smile playing on his lips as he scanned the room for a spot where they could settle in. His kind brown eyes met Ava's briefly, communicating a silent hope that tonight would somehow rekindle the flame that once burned so fiercely between them.

"Here," Ethan gestured toward a vacant table near the dance floor, his voice almost lost in the swell of music and chatter.

"Perfect," Ava replied, but her gaze was already drifting beyond the table, to the shifting mass of bodies on the dance floor. She felt a pull in her chest, an unspoken yearning that had lain dormant.

Without a word, Ethan took their cue and veered off toward the bar, his form momentarily swallowed by the crowd. He flagged down the bartender with a practiced wave, ordering drinks with a charm that had once made Ava fall for him so hard. But now, as she watched his back, she tasted the familiar tang of dissatisfaction at the back of her throat.

"Come on, let's dance," James said, his voice a low murmur, his hand light on the small of her back.

Ava nodded, surrendering to the moment, and allowing James to guide her through the maze of tables and chairs. As she stepped onto the dance floor, her body began to move instinctively with the rhythm, her steps matching the beat as if it were a pulse through her veins.

From the bar, Ethan watched, a glass of whiskey cradled in his hand. With each sip, he tried to drown the discomfort that gnawed at him, the jealousy that clouded his vision. He remained rooted to his stool, a silent sentinel, knowing deep down that he had promised to give Ava what she needed, even if it meant watching her in another man's arms.

On the dance floor, Ava cast a final glance back at Ethan, her eyes tracing the familiar contours of his face. She saw love there, but also pain—a silent testimony to the complexity of their shared journey. Then she turned away, her body moving closer to James as if drawn by a magnetic force that she didn't have the strength—or the desire—to resist.

The floor beneath Ava's heels vibrated with the twang of guitars and the rhythmic stomp of boots. James' hands found their place on her waist, firm yet tender as if he were claiming territory long sought after. She tilted her head back slightly, surrendering to the melody that seemed to speak directly to her soul, her body syncing with James' in a dance that felt both ancient and exhilaratingly new.

His touch sparked a current that traveled through her veins, igniting a flame that had been meticulously kindled over countless glances and whispered words. Each sway brought her closer into his orbit, her senses acutely aware of the heat radiating from his body, the scent of his cologne mingling with the rustic aroma of the bar. The music enveloped them, creating a cocoon that shuts out the rest of the world, leaving only the two of them in a dance as timeless as desire itself.

As the song climbed towards its peak, an electric fiddle crying out its high lonesome sound, James' grip tightened, pulling Ava even closer. It was a bold move, one that spoke of unspoken promises and nights spent yearning. Their eyes locked, green on blue, a silent conversation passing between them—a question posed by his gaze, answered by the slight parting of her lips.

At that moment, as the final notes soared, James leaned in, his lips finding hers with an urgency that left no room for hesitation. The kiss was a conflagration, a passionate declaration that consumed them both. Ava's fingers curled into the fabric of his shirt, anchoring herself to this anchor in the storm of sensation that threatened to sweep her away. Her heart pounded against her chest, a drumbeat in harmony with the pulsing rhythm of the song.

Their connection was a living thing, fierce and demanding as if the very air they breathed was charged with the electricity of their combined energies. The world around them faded, the dancers, the clinking glasses, even the plaintive wail of the country ballad—they all dissolved into nothingness. In their place was the overwhelming intensity of Ava and James, entwined in a kiss that was more than just physical—it was the merging of souls that had danced around each other for far too long.

Ethan's fingers tightened around the cool glass, a bead of condensation rolling down to meet his hand as he watched Ava with James. The thrumming bass of the country tune vibrated through the bar, yet it was the silent rhythm of Ava's body moving against another that seemed to resonate within him, each beat a dull thud against the walls of his heart. He could feel the weight of their history together pressing down on him—a history now being rewritten in the shadowed corners of the dance floor.

A flicker of discomfort danced across his features, the muscles in his jaw clenching as his eyes traced the familiar curve of Ava's smile, a smile that now bloomed for someone else. Jealousy nipped at him with sharp teeth, but Ethan swallowed it down, the bitter tang of beer mingling with the sting of unspoken regret. This was his choice, a path he had agreed to tread for the sake of Ava's happiness, no matter how much it gnawed at his insides.

Meanwhile, Ava was a flame, her emerald eyes alight with a fire kindled by James' kiss. The flush on her cheeks spoke volumes, her breath coming in quicker tides as she leaned into James, her voice barely more than a whisper over the cacophony of music and chatter. "Don't stop," she urged, the words laced with a hunger that had long been dormant. Each word was an invitation, a plea for liberation from the confines of the ordinary that had held her captive.

"Take me further," Ava breathed out, her lips close to James' ear, her intent clear as crystal. Her desire was a palpable force, an electric current that sought an outlet. In her plea was the echo of every silent night spent lying awake next to Ethan, the man she loved yet who could not ignite the spark that James now fanned into a blazing inferno.

From his vantage point, Ethan's gaze never wavered from Ava, even as the heat of the moment etched itself into his memory, a scorching brand upon the canvas of their shared life. The sight of her surrendering to her desires was both a torment and a balm, knowing she found in James what he could not give her. There, at the bar, with the ghost of their love watching over him, Ethan made his silent vow: to watch, to endure, and to allow Ava the freedom she craved, even if it meant weathering the storm alone.

Ava felt the shift in James' touch, a deliberate glide from the polite safety of her back to the daring crest of her buttocks. The change was subtle yet deliberate, a silent acknowledgment of her whispered invitation. It sent a cascade of shivers racing down her spine, each one igniting sparks that seemed to leap beneath her skin, awakening every nerve ending with a promise of what could be.

Her body, as if fluent in this wordless dialogue, responded instinctively. Her hips found a rhythm against his, a dance of their own amidst the twang of guitars and the beat of the drum. Each press of her body against his was a language she hadn't spoken in years, one of raw desire and unspoken needs. It was a dance that spoke of more than just movement; it was a sensuous conversation, an intimate exchange between two beings caught in a moment of pure connection.

The provocative sway of their hips became a testament to Ava's reawakened passion, a sensual echo of the hunger that had been simmering within her. She moved with purpose, allowing herself to melt into the music and James, forgetting the world, forgetting the watchful eyes of Ethan at the bar. It was just her and James, moving together in a dance that blurred the lines between boldness and vulnerability, between spectator and participant, between what was expected and what was desired.

James's fingers, emboldened by Ava's silent plea for more, began a tender exploration that seemed to chart unknown territories even in this public setting. They traced the upper swell of her backside with a possessive yet reverent touch, drawing invisible lines that felt like they were searing into her flesh. Every nerve ending flared beneath his fingertips, and Ava felt as if she were not just standing there on the dance floor but also perched on the precipice of some great and thrilling unknown.

Much like Charlene's growing awareness of the void in her wedded bliss, Ava's skin hummed with realization, acknowledging the depth of desire she had tried to lock away. James' touch was awakening something primal within her—a need that demanded recognition after years of being tucked neatly behind her confidence and control.

As the music swirled around them, the stinging guitar riffs and pounding drums of the country ballad became mere echoes compared to the symphony of sensations coursing through Ava's veins. The clamor of the bar, the chatter, and the laughter of other patrons—all of it receded into a distant murmur. It was as though a hazy veil had descended, separating Ava and James from the rest of the world, leaving them suspended in their cocoon of heat and passion.

The connection between them pulsed and grew, almost palpable in its intensity, as their bodies continued to move to the rhythm of the haunting melody. With each sway, their shared desire wound tighter, spiraling into an exquisite tension that sought release. Ava's breath hitched, her emerald eyes half-closed in a languid gaze that spoke volumes of the pleasure she found in James' embrace.

At that moment, Ava realized how starved she had been for this kind of connection—for the all-consuming blaze that now licked at her insides, threatening to consume her whole. James, with his knowing hands and intoxicating nearness, was no longer just a man she was dancing with; he was the embodiment of every carnal fantasy she'd dared to entertain, now brought vividly to life in the dim light of the local bar.

Ethan's hand clenched around the cold glass, moisture beading and rolling down its curved side. His knuckles whitened, a stark contrast to the tawny liquid contained within. From his solitary post at the bar, he watched—each glance felt like sandpaper against his conscience. Ava, with her raven hair reflecting the dim lights overhead, was a vision that stirred him always. But now, it was James' hands tracing the landscape of her body, not his own.

The struggle within Ethan was palpable, a tempest of jealousy clashing against the vow he'd made to himself—to see her fulfilled in ways he had failed to manage. For five years, he'd been blind to the void in their bedroom, deaf to the silent pleas whispered by her body language. Only when confronted with the undeniable truth did he awaken to Ava's needs—needs that sent her spiraling into another's arms on a dance floor thrumming with raw energy.

Ava's silhouette melded with James', her hips swaying in time with his, undulating like waves upon a moonlit shore. The thrall of the music seemed to possess them, guiding their movements as they pushed the boundaries of public decency. There was a fervor in the way she tilted her head back, exposing the elegant line of her throat—a silent scream to the universe, a declaration of her awakening.

As their passion crested, the space between them grew charged, a current that threaded through the crowd and zapped straight into Ethan's core. He saw in every dip and rise of their bodies a symphony of unspoken words, a dance of longing that had languished too long in the shadows. Their connection was undeniable, a magnetic pull so strong that it left no room for doubt or denial.

Ethan swallowed the bitterness rising in his throat, the taste of his insecurity mingling with the aged whiskey. Each movement Ava shared with James was a testament to her exploration, a journey he had inadvertently mapped out even as he stood static, a bystander to her voyage. His heart thundered a rhythm akin to the beat pulsating through the bar, a staccato reminder of the emotional odyssey that lay ahead.

A final chord strummed through the air, a vibrating echo that lingered like the touch of a lover's caress. Ava and James stilled, their bodies pressed together in the aftermath of the dance, hearts pounding an echo to the fading music. Breathless whispers of desire clung to their lips as they pulled apart, the reluctant space between them charged with the electricity of unsaid promises.

Ava's emerald eyes shimmered with an unquenched yearning as she glanced back at James, her body still resonating with the rhythm of their shared heat. She moved away, each step toward the bar a small journey back to a reality she wasn't sure she wanted to inhabit. Her hair, dark as a raven's wing, swayed with a silent cadence, a stark contrast to the cacophony of the bar.

As she neared Ethan, his silhouette etched against the dim lighting, she noted the rigidity in his posture, the way his hand clenched around his glass. His warm smile was absent, replaced by a taut line that spoke volumes of the battle raging within him. Their gaze met, and Ava read the turmoil etched in the depths of his brown eyes, a maelstrom of love entwined with pain.

Her heart clenched, recognizing the silent plea for understanding and the shadow of hurt that had crept into their life together, much like the creeping chill of a foggy dawn that seeps through the windows of an otherwise warm home. For a moment, they simply looked at each other, words unnecessary and yet desperately needed, the air around them thick with the things left unsaid and feelings barely contained.

Ava slid into the seat opposite Ethan, her skin still humming from the press of James's body against hers. The bar's din receded to a low buzz in her ears, the world narrowing down to the space between her and her husband. She noticed the clench of his jaw, the distress muted but unmistakable in his eyes—a silent testament to the feelings roiling beneath his calm exterior.

"Are you okay?" she asked, the query gentle, almost hesitant as if she were afraid to unravel the fragile thread holding him together.

Ethan attempted a smile, but it faltered, revealing the cracks in his composure. "Yeah," he lied, and Ava knew it for what it was—an armor he donned out of love, a shield raised to protect not himself but her. He took a sip from his drink, a measured action that spoke of his need to ground himself, to remain the steadfast figure he had always been in their life together.

She reached across the table, her fingers brushing against his hand. The contact was light, yet it carried the weight of all the unspoken emotions that had steadily accumulated over time. Like a dam straining against the pressure of an ever-rising flood, she felt the precarious balance they had maintained begin to tremble, threatening to give way.

The air seemed to thicken with tension, heavy with anticipation of the unknown. Ava could sense the precipice on which they stood, the edge of a chasm that beckoned them toward a future filled with uncertainty and the potential for both exquisite joy and profound heartache.

In the charged silence, Ava realized the dance floor encounter wasn't just a fleeting moment of passion—it was a catalyst, a spark igniting a fire that would either consume or illuminate the path ahead. As she looked into Ethan's troubled gaze, she acknowledged the necessity of the journey they were about to embark upon—a journey not just of physical exploration but of emotional vulnerability and self-discovery.

Their reality had shifted, subtly altered by the gravity of desire and the complexities of the human heart. And though the way forward was fraught with the possibility of pain, Ava understood that the truest form of love demanded bravery, the courage to face the depths of one's soul and emerge, perhaps changed, but more authentic than ever before.

# Chapter Seven – The Next Test

Ethan's fingers trembled slightly as they hovered over the phone's keypad, a visible testament to the tumultuous storm brewing within. He drew in a deep breath, steadying his hand before pressing the numbers with deliberate precision. The line buzzed for a moment, connecting him to a voice that carried the promise of anonymity and discretion.

"Sunset Motel, how may I assist you?" came the distant reply, impersonal and detached.

"Hi, I need to book a room for tonight," Ethan said, his voice betraying none of the chaos that threatened to spill from his chest.

"Of course," the clerk answered. "Name for the reservation?"

"Ethan Myers," he replied, and after a short exchange of details, he added softly, "It'll be under James Harris, though." The name felt foreign on his tongue, like a bitter pill he had to swallow.

"Reservation is all set, Mr. Myers. We'll see Mr. Harris tonight."

"Thank you," Ethan managed, ending the call with a click that seemed to echo in the silence of the room.

Ava watched him from across the space, her emerald eyes holding depths of understanding and something else — a yearning that made his heart clench. She moved towards him with that confident stride, exuding an air of certainty that had first drawn him to her. Her raven hair caught the light, casting shadows across her high cheekbones.

"Ethan," she began, her voice calm and measured, "will you drive us to the motel? It would mean... it would mean a lot to me."

He looked up into her eyes, searching for the familiar warmth he knew so well. Instead, he found a complex tapestry of desire and regret that mirrored his internal struggle. There was no escaping the reality of their situation; Ava needed more than what he could give her alone, and he loved her too much to deny her this exploration.

"Of course, I'll take you," Ethan said, the words feeling heavy on his tongue. His heart pounded with a mixture of anticipation for her happiness and anxiety for his aching soul. He forced a warm smile, one that didn't quite reach his brown eyes, but enough to reassure her.

"Thank you," Ava whispered, her lips curving into a subtle smile that showcased her dimple, a feature he had always adored. She reached out, her touch gentle on his arm — a silent thank you that spoke volumes.

Ethan nodded, keeping his emotions carefully in check. A sense of duty mingled with love propelled him forward. He would see this through for her, even if it meant driving straight into the heart of his deepest fears.

Ava slid into the backseat with a fluid grace, her every movement laced with an unspoken promise. James followed suit, the door closing behind him with a soft thud that felt final, a seal on the decision made. Their bodies were close, the space in Ethan's car suddenly feeling much smaller. They turned towards each other, their gazes locking in silent conversation, electric with desire.

In the driver's seat, Ethan's hands closed around the steering wheel, his fingers curling until his knuckles stood out stark and white against the dark leather. He drew in a deep breath, trying to calm the storm of emotions raging inside him. Love, anger, pain, and a fierce protective instinct for Ava all clashed within the confines of his heart.

For five years, Ethan had prided himself on being the man Ava could rely on, her steadfast partner. But now, as he sat there with his wife in the arms of another, he couldn't help but question what had gone missing between them, what essential spark he had failed to kindle that James could so easily ignite.

With each shallow breath, Ethan fought to steady the tremor in his hands, to appear composed. He was committed to supporting Ava's journey, even if it meant driving through the night, chasing shadows of doubt with each passing streetlight. The hum of the engine, as he turned the key, was a small mercy, drowning out the whisper of his insecurities.

Ava's green eyes glistened under the dull light as she rested her head on James' shoulder, their bodies molded together in sinful celebration. She turned to look at Ethan, her expression a blend of desire and invitation. He watched her lips curl into a smirk, her tongue darting out seductively to wet them. His heart raced and his arousal pulsed, humming loud enough for him to feel it throb beneath the restrictive confinement of his pants.

James took that moment to slip a hand beneath Ava's skirt which had ridden up indecently high. Ethan saw Ava's chest heave against her tight blouse as James' fingers ventured higher, touching the edges of her lacy panties. From where Ethan sat, he could clearly discern how soaked they were. The sight made his mouth water with yearning —an aching sense of longing that threatened to consume him whole.

He noticed James' fingers glisten with Ava's juices as he withdrew them from her swollen pussy. An animalistic growl escaped James's lips before he plunged back into Ava, the smack of flesh echoing through the car.

Ava whimpered, pressing her lush body against James, begging for more while Ethan increased his rhythm, matching the torturous pace James was setting. His thumb circled his sensitive tip making him buck into his hand. His pleasure-ridden moans blended with Ava's cries of ecstasy—spurring him to pump harder and faster.

Her nails clawed at James' arm as a climax rolled over her. Her shuddering whimpers filling the tight space inside the car made Ethan grunt—his balls pulled tight signaling his impending release. As Ava descended from her orgasmic high, Ethan felt his seed spurting over his hand —sticky and warm.

His chest heaved as pleasure washed over him—leaving him feeling both satisfied and empty. He continued watching them in silence—a spectator lost in their world of forbidden desires and sinful pleasures that promised many more nights fraught with illicit escapades.

Ava's quiet moan drifted forward, entwining with the hum of the engine—a siren's call that punctuated the silence of the car and reverberated through Ethan's very bones. He pressed down on the accelerator, willing the motel to come into view sooner, desperate to end this journey of torment and truth that they had all embarked upon.

The neon sign of the motel flickered into view, its garish glow slicing through the darkness and offering a beacon of finality. Ethan's breath came in short, sharp bursts as he guided the car into a parking space, the gravel crunching under the tires like a harsh whisper. He killed the engine, the sudden silence in the car thick with unspoken words and fervent anticipation.

Ava's hand was clasped tightly in James's, their fingers entwined as if they were holding onto each other for dear life. The moment the vehicle stopped, they seemed to spring to life, their embrace igniting with urgency. Ethan watched, his heart thrumming against his ribs, as Ava threw open the door and almost tumbled out, her lover following in one fluid motion. Their bodies melded together, lips locked in a fierce kiss that spoke of hunger too long denied.

Ethan sat frozen, a silent spectator to the passion he had facilitated but could not partake in. He observed Ava's back arching, pressing herself against James, their hands roaming with feverish intensity. It was a dance of desire he knew all too well, yet it was choreographed with steps unfamiliar to him.

With a swift movement, Ava and James broke apart just enough to stumble toward the motel room, their need for privacy now outweighing their need for contact. The keycard flashed in James's hand before the door clicked open, swallowing them into a room lit by the soft, expectant glow of lamplight.

Inside, the world is reduced to the space between them. Clothes fell away like discarded shields, revealing the raw truth of skin and sinew.

James's hands traced the curve of Ava's spine, eliciting a shiver that ran down her body, igniting every nerve ending with a promise of ecstasy. Her emerald eyes, usually so commanding, now shimmered with a vulnerability and a fierce desire that seared through the air between them.

As they came together, the room seemed to pulse with the rhythm of their union—a crescendo of shared breaths and whispered names. Ava surrendered to the sensations that James drew forth from her, each touch rekindling embers into a roaring blaze. They moved with a synchronicity that bordered on primal, each thrust, each gasp a testament to the carnal feast they indulged in.

And there, in the dimly lit room, the boundaries of their bodies blurred, the passion they unleashed was as intense as it was profound, sculpting a moment in time where nothing else existed but the fierce tide of their lovemaking.

With a mechanical motion, Ethan cut the engine and sat motionless behind the wheel, his gaze fixed on the motel door that had closed behind Ava and James. The silence of the car was deafening, wrapping around him like a shroud. He could feel every beat of his heart, each one echoing Ava's departure further into another's arms.

Ethan's hands trembled slightly as they came to rest in his lap, the warmth of the steering wheel lingering on his skin like an accusation. Jealousy gnawed at his insides, a bitter and unwelcome guest, while longing whispered sweet memories of what once was theirs alone. His mind churned with images he conjured and those he dreaded – Ava's laughter, her emerald eyes alight with passion, now shared with another.

He drew in a deep breath, trying to steady himself against the onslaught of emotions that threatened to overwhelm him. It was a deep sense of loss that settled heavily in his chest, a realization that the intimacy he and Ava had woven over five years might be unraveling thread by thread.

And then, in his mind sounds began to drift through the thin walls, barely audible yet unmistakably charged with pleasure. Moans of ecstasy that should have been private now spilled into the night, carrying across the short expanse to where Ethan sat in his self-imposed exile. The murmurs were a melody of forbidden desire, a harmony created by two bodies that were not his own.

Ethan squeezed his eyes shut, willing away the images that the sounds painted so vividly in his mind. But his resolve was ironclad; this was Ava's exploration, her journey to rediscover a part of herself she felt she had lost. And though it carved into him, leaving raw edges that ached with every pulsating note of pleasure that reached his ears, he would not falter.

In the stillness of the car, with the chorus of Ava's newfound ecstasy ringing in the background, Ethan faced the tempest within. His commitment to support her, despite the cost to his own heart, was the one anchor keeping him from being swept away by the storm of jealousy, longing, and loss.

Ethan's fingers tapped an erratic rhythm against the steering wheel, each beat a sharp counterpoint to the muffled symphony of passion that filtered through the car windows. He tried to focus on the cool night air that caressed his face, but it was laden with the scent of possibility and change, sensations that once seemed reserved for young lovers, not for a man watching his wife reclaim her sensuality from the arms of another.

The motel sign flickered intermittently, casting shadows that danced across Ethan's features—shadows that mirrored the dark waves of doubt cresting in his mind. For five years, he had believed their marriage was the epitome of fulfillment, yet here he was, parked outside a nondescript room where Ava sought the answers to questions he hadn't known she'd been asking.

His gaze lingered on the closed door, behind which lay a world he was barred from entering—a world where Ava's emerald eyes likely shimmered with a fervor he had only glimpsed but never fully ignited. His heart wrestled with visions of her raven hair fanned out across unfamiliar sheets, her poise undone by raw desire, her calm certainty replaced by breathless whispers.

The reality that he could no longer be her sole harbor, her exclusive provider of pleasure, settled like a weight in his stomach. The fabric of their union, once seamless, now revealed its frayed edges, and Ethan grappled with the fear that each thread might come loose, unraveling the tapestry of their shared history.

As the night deepened around him, the silence within the car grew heavy, pregnant with the unspoken aftermath of this pivotal night. Would Ava return to him satiated, her exploratory flames quenched, or would her hunger only grow, widening the gap between them? Would his open palms, extended in support, be enough to bridge the distance, or would they simply wave farewell to the remnants of love transformed?

With each second that ticked by, the questions multiplied, leaving Ethan suspended in a limbo of what-ifs and maybes. The chapter of their lives was drawing to a close, but the next page was blank, unwritten, leaving the reader—and Ethan—to wonder how the ink of Ava, James, and his own choices would script their tomorrow.

# Chapter Eight – Emotional Turmoil

Ava perched on the edge of the plush velvet couch, the fabric's softness a stark contrast to the rigidity of her posture. The living room, once a sanctuary of marital bliss, now felt like a courtroom where the echoes of last night's indiscretions hung heavy in the air. She crossed one leg over the other, her foot tapping an anxious rhythm against the hardwood floor.

Ethan, sitting beside her, was a picture of silent turmoil. His fingers drummed against his knee, a metronome to Ava's nervous energy. He glanced at her, the hurt in his brown eyes tempered by a flicker of understanding that betrayed his inner conflict. Five years into their marriage and here they were, navigating uncharted territories of pain and longing.

He drew in a deep breath, his chest rising visibly as he mustered the courage to breach the silence. "Ava," he began, his voice steadier than his trembling hands suggested, "I can't pretend I know how to feel about...about what happened with James."

Ava's emerald eyes, usually so full of purpose, now swam with complexities she couldn't articulate. Ethan's confession, raw and vulnerable, cut through her defenses, reminding her why she fell for him all those years ago.

"Last night," Ethan continued, each word measured and laced with the weight of their shared history, "it changed something between us. And I can't help but feel..."

His sentence trailed off, leaving his emotions suspended in the space between them. Ava reached out tentatively, her fingertips brushing against his hand, seeking to bridge the gap that had formed overnight with a single, transgressive act.

Ava felt the couch shift beneath her as Ethan leaned forward, his elbows bracing against his thighs. She watched his jaw clench, a physical manifestation of the emotional maelstrom he was weathering.

His kind eyes, usually so full of warmth, now glistened with a sheen that spoke of deep inner turmoil.

"Talk to me, Ava," he implored, his voice betraying the trepidation that laced every syllable. "Was it everything you hoped for?"

The question hung in the air, thick and heavy, pressing down on Ava's shoulders like the weight of their five-year history together. In the stillness of their living room, she could hear the faint ticking of the wall clock, each second magnified by the gravity of the moment.

She swallowed hard, her throat tight with emotion. The desire to explore that had been simmering within her for years, unspoken but ever-present, now seemed both vindicated and burdensome. How could she explain the tangled web of satisfaction and guilt that the night with James had woven inside her?

"Exploration comes with its own set of revelations," Ava said carefully, choosing her words like a navigator plotting a course through stormy waters. Her gaze did not waver from Ethan's face, seeking pardon and understanding in equal measure.

Ethan absorbed her response, his expression a canvas of complexity. He understood—of course, he understood—her need to venture beyond the boundaries they had silently drawn around their relationship. But understanding did not stem the flow of his pain any more than it could staunch his curiosity.

"Did he give you what I couldn't?" he asked, the curiosity in his voice competing with the undercurrent of fear that maybe, just maybe, he had lost something irreplaceable.

Ava reached for his hand, the contact grounding them amidst the swirling chaos of their emotions. As their fingers intertwined, she found herself anchored not just by the solidity of his grasp, but also by the resilience of their bond.

In the silence that followed, Ava knew that their journey ahead would be fraught with challenges and uncertainties. Yet, in the act of facing them side by side, they were forging a new intimacy, one that held the promise of rekindled passion and rediscovered connection.

Ava caught the tremble in Ethan's lips, a subtle quiver that betrayed his effort to remain stoic. His eyes, warm pools of melted chocolate, searched hers for something—forgiveness, perhaps, or reassurance. She felt the weight of his gaze, heavy with questions unasked and feelings unvoiced.

"Five years," Ava whispered, her voice barely more than a breath as she released the truth that had clawed at her insides. "It was... it was like nothing I've experienced in five years."

The words hung between them, raw and exposed. Her confession sliced through the air, an invisible blade severing layers of comfort and routine they had both wrapped around themselves. Guilt mingled with the afterglow of satisfaction, creating a conflicting storm within her. She watched as the edges of Ethan's smile crumbled, leaving behind a pained grimace that he quickly masked.

Ethan swallowed hard, his Adam's apple bobbing with the effort. He blinked slowly, once, twice, allowing the hurt to wash over him before pushing it aside. His hand, still clasped with Ava's, tightened its grip—a silent vow that he was there, present in the pain, willing to wade through it for her, for them.

"Okay," he murmured, the single word carrying the weight of his love, his jealousy, and his resolve. It was his commitment to understand, to support her in her quest for fulfillment even if it carved into his own heart. Ava could see it in the way his jaw set, a determined line that spoke of his inner strength, and in the steadfastness of his gaze that refused to look away from what they were facing together.

Ava inhaled deeply, the air filling her lungs as if to buoy her courage. The room, once a sanctuary of shared whispers and laughter, now held a different kind of energy—one charged with the electricity of unspoken desires and unveiled truths. She glanced at Ethan, his features etched with the turmoil of their confession, yet his presence was a steady force beside her.

"Call him," she said, her voice a decisive whisper that seemed to vibrate through the stillness of the room. "Call James. I want... we need to invite him here again."

Ethan's reaction was immediate, his eyes snapping up to meet hers. Surprise flickered there, like the sudden flare of a match in darkness, illuminating the contours of his face. He searched her eyes, those emerald pools that had always been a source of strength and mystery to him. In them, he saw the reflection of her growing confidence, the ember of her curiosity fanned into flame by the night before.

"Here?" Ethan's voice cracked slightly, betraying the storm of emotions brewing inside of him—jealousy, hurt, but also an undeniable intrigue. His heart raced, keeping tempo with the thoughts swirling in his mind. Ava, his Ava, was evolving before his eyes, shedding layers of restraint in pursuit of her awakening.

"Yes," Ava affirmed, her lips parting to reveal the subtle dimple on one cheek, a testament to her resolve. "In our bed. Where we've dreamed together, cried together... it's time we explore together too."

Ethan looked at her, really looked—as though seeing her for the first time. Her poise was unshakable, her request an open door to a path they could tread side by side. And although fear gnawed at the edges of his composure, Ethan recognized the need to support her exploration, to be a part of her journey toward fulfillment, just as she had been part of his for so many years.

"Okay," Ethan breathed out, the word less of a surrender and more of an acquiescence to the inevitable evolution of their desires. He understood then, perhaps not fully, but enough to know that this was not just about inviting another man into their marriage bed—it was about inviting a new chapter in their lives, one where Ava's boldness would lead them into uncharted territories of passion and intimacy.

Ethan's fingers hovered above the sleek surface of his phone, a slight tremor betraying the turmoil beneath his calm exterior. He was about to cross a threshold from which there would be no return, dialing into a future where the rules of their union were rewritten by the hands of another man. The weight of the decision pressed upon him as he took in a slow, steadying breath.

Ava observed Ethan with an intensity that seemed to anchor him in the moment. Her gaze did not waver, her emerald eyes reflecting a fervent blend of apprehension and desire. Each second stretched out between them, thick with unspoken questions and the echo of heartbeats syncing in shared vulnerability.

With a resolve that came from somewhere deep within, Ethan made contact with the cool screen, each tap sending ripples through the stillness of the room. Ava's lips parted slightly, a silent gasp that acknowledged the gravity of what was unfolding. She leaned forward, the subtle arch of her body speaking volumes about her longing, her readiness for the flames that might soon consume them both.

The line clicked, connected, and the world was reduced to the sound of a ringtone pulsing in the space between them. Ethan held Ava's gaze, searching for strength in the depths of her certainty. Their breaths mingled, a silent symphony of anticipation playing out as they awaited the voice that would seal their fate.

"Hello?" James' voice crackled through the speaker, laced with an undercurrent of eagerness that betrayed his intrigue at the unexpected call.

Ethan's throat tightened, a tumultuous mix of emotions swirling within him as he uttered the words that would invite another man into the sacred space of their marriage. "James, it's Ethan. Ava and I... we were wondering if you'd be open to meeting again."

On the couch, Ava sat motionless but for the faint tremor that danced through her fingertips. She watched Ethan closely, her verdant eyes shimmering with the complexity of her emotions—the thrill of her desires clashing with the nerves that chewed at the edges of her resolve.

The silence on the other end of the line stretched taut, and for a brief moment, Ava felt the piercing sting of vulnerability. The possibility of rejection loomed over her, a specter threatening to douse the flames of her newfound boldness.

"Sure," came James' response, a note of suppressed zeal threading through his tone. "I had a feeling this might not have been a one-time thing."

Ava exhaled a breath she hadn't realized she'd been holding, relief mingling with a heat that began to unfurl within her. Her gaze remained fixed on Ethan, reading the waves of conflict passing over his features even as he navigated the conversation with a calm she knew must have cost him dearly.

"Great," Ethan said, a practiced smile touching his lips though it failed to reach his eyes. "We'll talk details later."

As Ethan ended the call and set down the phone, the room was engulfed in a pensive quietude. Ava's heart throbbed against her ribcage, a symphony of nervous excitement playing out beneath her skin. Her mind raced with visions of what was to come—sensations, touches, the intertwining of passion and pleasure that awaited.

Ethan's thumb pressed the disconnect button with a finality that echoed in the stillness of their living room. The phone slipped from his hand onto the cushion beside him, an insignificant piece of technology that had just set the course for events unimaginable mere weeks ago. He turned to face Ava, his brown eyes clouded with a tumult of emotions—each one battling for dominance.

"James will come," he said, his voice steady despite the turmoil that Ava knew was churning inside him. His jaw tensed as he delivered the words, betraying the inner conflict between his desire to please her and the unease of sharing her once more.

Ava felt her pulse quicken, her breaths becoming shallow. The reality of Ethan's acquiescence sent a jolt through her body, igniting a fire that began to spread with reckless abandon. Her desires, long suppressed in the confines of monogamy, were pushing through the surface, demanding to be sated yet again.

"Thank you," she managed to whisper, her voice laced with a complexity of gratitude and passion. It was more than just a thank you for making the call; it was an acknowledgment of his sacrifice, of his love that was willing to bend in ways many would not understand.

Her emerald eyes held his gaze, searching for signs of regret or anger, but instead, she found resolve. Ethan's acceptance of her needs, even when they diverged from his own, wrapped around her like a warm embrace, intensifying the anticipation of James's arrival.

He'd done it. Ethan had stepped into the unknown, guided by a love that was selfless and raw, and for that, Ava admired him all the more. With each passing second, the air between them vibrated with silent recognition of the threshold they had crossed together—a journey that would test the very fabric of their union.

In this space of waiting, Ava's heart danced to the rhythm of a future unfolding, a canvas of carnal exploration painted with bold strokes of trust and openness. She allowed herself to feel every beat, every surge of excitement, as the promise of fulfillment beckoned, closer now than ever before.

Ethan reached across the expanse of their shared history, his hand seeking hers, an anchor in the tumultuous sea of emotions that churned within them both. His fingers found Ava's, and like a key to a lock, they intertwined effortlessly, a testament to the intimacy that still thrived amidst uncertainty. Their physical connection was as natural as breathing, yet now it carried the weight of unspoken promises and uncharted territories.

In the gentle clasp of Ethan's hand, Ava felt the subtle tremors of his apprehension, the warmth of his love that had always been her beacon through the fog of doubt. She marveled at the paradox of strength and vulnerability that emanated from his touch, the same hands that had once vowed to cherish her above all else now poised to venture into the shadowy depths of her desires.

The living room, their sanctuary of shared memories, seemed to hold its breath, bearing witness to the silent conversation that passed between them. Ava studied the lines etched into Ethan's palm, each one a roadmap of their life together, intersecting and diverging in a pattern that told stories of joy and struggle, of holding on and letting go.

As their eyes locked, the world outside faded away, leaving only the reality of their bond, forged in love and now bending towards the unknown. Ava saw the flicker of questions in Ethan's deep brown gaze, the same queries that echoed in her own heart—would this journey fortify their union or would it be the unraveling thread?

Yet, for all the fears that whispered of potential loss, there was also a silent understanding that growth often demanded risk, and that fulfillment sometimes lay beyond the boundaries of convention. And so, with their fingers laced together, they stood on the precipice of change, ready to step into the future, whatever it may hold.

Their shared breath became a rhythm, a cadence that pulsed with the courage to face what lay ahead. Together, they acknowledged the challenges, the risks, and the sheer audacity of the path they were about to tread—a path of discovery, not just of flesh and pleasure, but of the very essence that bound them as one.

# Chapter Nine – Breaking Point

Ava's heels clicked against the hardwood floor with purpose as she made her way towards Ethan, who sat pensively in the dimly lit living room. The soft glow of the table lamp cast shadows on his thoughtful face, further accentuating the kind brown eyes that always seemed to see right through her. He looked up, a warm smile ready on his lips, but it faltered at the sight of her expression—a blend of determination and resolve.

"Love, I need your help getting things ready for James," Ava said, her voice steady like the unyielding current of a river. It was that same tone she used when making decisions that brooked no argument, the same one that drew him to her years ago, filled with confidence and clarity.

For a fleeting moment, Ethan's heart stuttered in his chest. The request hung heavily in the air between them, laden with unspoken implications. He had known this day would come; he could see it in the distant look that sometimes clouded her emerald eyes, a silent yearning for something more, something he had struggled to provide. Now, faced with the reality of aiding her in preparing for another man, Ethan felt an internal tug-of-war—his desire to make her happy warring with the ache in his soul.

"Are you sure about this?" His voice came out softer than intended, a mere whisper of the turmoil brewing within.

"Yes, I am," she replied, the hint of a dimple on her cheek doing nothing to soften the gravity of her words. There was no hesitation, no flicker of doubt in her steady gaze. She had made up her mind.

Ethan took a deep breath, his hands unconsciously clenching and unclenching as he grappled with the emotions swirling inside him. Yet, despite the hurt, despite the jealousy that threatened to consume him, he loved her. And if this was what she needed—to explore the depths of her desires, to seek fulfillment in ways he hadn't been able to provide—he wouldn't stand in her way.

"Okay," he finally conceded, the word tasting bitter on his tongue. "I'll help."

Her smile widened just a fraction, a silent thank you, but Ethan couldn't help but feel that with each step they took down this path, a piece of their bond chipped away, leaving behind a future uncertain and fraught with heartache.

Ava's voice cut through the silence, crisp and authoritative. "The sheets in the master bedroom need changing. Something soft, something that feels like an embrace. Make sure they're fresh for James."

Ethan's fingers twitched at his sides, betraying the tremor that had taken root deep within him. He crossed the threshold into the sanctuary of their shared intimacy, now to be laid out for another. His hands found the linen closet with practiced ease, yet they fumbled with the folded edges of the cotton sheets, sheets that whispered of nights spent in passion, now relegated to mere fabric.

"Will you need anything else?" Ethan asked his back to her, a thin veil of composure barely cloaking the quiver in his tone.

"Just make sure everything is perfect," came Ava's reply, each word hanging heavy in the air between them. Her voice had become hard and demanding.

He nodded to an empty room, his acknowledgment of her command lost in the void she'd left behind. The weight of the task at hand pressed down on him, each step towards the master bathroom a journey through a minefield of memories—each one a testament to what was and what might never be again.

Gathering the necessary supplies from the hallway cupboard—a cache of cleaning agents and sponges, unused to such somber duty—Ethan's grip tightened around the handle of the mop bucket. His heart echoed a similar cadence, a dull throb against the cage of his ribs, as he filled it with water and bleach, the acrid scent unable to cleanse the sour taste of his reality.

The tile gleamed under his meticulous care, each stroke of the scrub brush a balm to the chaos of his thoughts. If he could but polish away the evidence of his faltering, perhaps then the mirror would cease its mockery, no longer reflecting a man fractured by his insecurities.

He worked in silence, the only sound the slosh of water and his labored breaths. The pristine nature of the bathroom stood in stark contrast to the turmoil that churned within him—a tempest of love and loss, swirling into the abyss of the unknown.

Ethan twisted the faucet, a gush of steaming water cascading into the tub with a roar that mimicked the rush of blood in his ears. Ava stood at the threshold of the bathroom, her silhouette framed by the dim light of the hallway. "Warm but not too hot," she instructed, the certainty in her voice slicing through the humid air.

"Of course," Ethan replied, the words barely audible over the drumming of the water. He watched the liquid rise, steam fogging the mirror and beading on his forehead. The scent of lavender bath oil filled the space as he poured it into the swirling vortex, each drop spreading out like the ripples of change about to disrupt the still surface of their lives.

Ava's gaze lingered on the bath, then shifted to Ethan, her emerald eyes reflecting an anticipation he wasn't permitted to share. She was preparing for another, yet it was Ethan's hands that orchestrated the prelude to her liaison.

"Thank you," she murmured, turning away, leaving Ethan clutching the edge of the sink. His heart pounded against his sternum, a rhythmic reminder of the role he'd been reduced to—facilitator of his heartache. He tried to focus on the soothing sound of the water, but it was no match for the cacophony of his racing thoughts.

As he adjusted the temperature, ensuring it adhered to Ava's specifications, he couldn't help but wonder if this was how it had felt for Charlene, those five years spent grappling with the silent void in her marriage. With every second that ticked closer to James' arrival, Ethan felt a kinship with that sense of something amiss, that gnawing ache of insufficiency that seemed to grow more pronounced with each task he performed for Ava's benefit—and his detriment.

Ava disrobed with a fluidity that seemed to leave no room for hesitation, her movements as deliberate as they had always been. With each layer she shed, the air grew thicker, weighted by the unspoken words between them. She stepped into the bath, the water embracing her form with a welcoming warmth. A sigh escaped her lips, not of contentment, but of resignation to the evening's script—a script in which Ethan felt like an understudy for a role he never coveted.

"Could you...?" Ava's voice trailed off, but her eyes held his, a silent plea echoing in their depths. It was a request that transcended the spoken word, one that reached into the recesses of their shared history, where intimacy once blossomed unrestrained.

Ethan approached, his hands betraying the internal chaos that seized him—jealousy, love, and an aching desire to reclaim what was slipping through his fingers. He dipped his hands into the lavender-scented water, gathering it in his palms before letting it cascade gently over Ava's shoulders. As he touched her skin, warm and soft beneath his quivering fingers, he fought against the tide of memories threatening to overwhelm him. The scent of her hair, the curve of her back—these were sacred verses in the love sonnets he had composed in the solitude of his heart.

"Here, let me," he murmured, taking the sponge and tracing the contours of her back with a tenderness that belied his crumbling facade. Each stroke was a word left unsaid, a stanza in their unfulfilled tale of passion and longing. His gaze lingered on the droplets of water that traced paths along her spine, paths he longed to follow with lips that ached to speak the truth.

The tension that hung between them was a palpable entity, a silent specter that observed the intimate charade with a knowing stare. Ava leaned back slightly into his touch, a quiet acknowledgment of their shared turmoil, yet Ethan could feel the distance between them—a chasm widened by unmet needs and unspoken grievances.

As his fingers worked through her raven-black hair, untangling knots with care that bordered on reverence, Ethan's thoughts raced with images of the night ahead. With every moment that passed, the reality of his situation bore down upon him, a cruel weight that pressed upon his chest, stealing the breath from his lungs. How much longer could he bear this torment? How much more of his heart was he willing to sacrifice at the altar of Ava's desires?

Yet still, he continued, his hands moving with a practiced ease that belied the chaos within. He would see this through, for her, until the final act played out and the curtain fell on the tragedy of their love.

The steam from the bath had begun to dissipate, a ghostly swirl fading into the cool air of the master bedroom. Ava rose, her skin glistening with droplets that clung to her like jewels, and she wrapped herself in a towel with a fluid grace that Ethan had always admired. Her eyes met his, emerald fires burning with an intensity that was both enthralling and intimidating.

"Choose something for me, Ethan," she said, her voice a velvet command that left no room for refusal. "Something that will make James unable to look away."

Ethan nodded, though each muscle in his body tensed at the task. He moved toward the wardrobe, the space where fabric and fantasy intertwined—a sartorial garden of Eden that now felt more like a minefield. His fingers brushed against silk, lace, and satin, materials that whispered promises of seduction and secrets yet to be unfurled.

With trembling hands, he selected a dress, the color of deep merlot, a provocative garment designed to cling to every curve, to suggest rather than reveal. It was a dress Ava had worn once before, on an anniversary that now seemed like a lifetime ago. He remembered how it had made him feel then—proud, desired, irrevocably in love. Now, the same dress was a symbol of his inadequacy, a reminder of the distance that had grown between them.

"Will this do?" His voice was barely above a whisper, choked by the rising tide of jealousy that threatened to consume him.

Ava approached, her bare feet silent on the plush carpet. She took the dress from him, her fingertips briefly brushing his. A spark of their old connection flared, and for a moment, Ethan allowed himself to hope. But as quickly as it came, it was extinguished by the cold draft of reality.

"Perfect," she affirmed, and the word cut through him sharper than any blade. Now how about the lingerie that will go under the dress? I believe that James prefers black with red lace trim. See if I have anything that would complement such a choice. Ethan chose a black lace bra with red lace trim, matching panties, and a garter belt with red accents. He also found black stockings with red lace detailing at the top to tie in with the overall theme.

As Ethan helps Ava into the black lace bra with red trim, fastening it at the back he a sense of nostalgia for their past intimacy. He hesitates a moment before attaching the garter belt, his touch lingering slightly longer than necessary, conveying unspoken emotions between them. As he helps her adjust the black stockings with red lace detailing, there's a palpable tension in the air, laden with unspoken words and memories.

She slipped into the dress with an ease that spoke of her familiarity with allure and its power. The fabric embraced her figure, the merlot hue a stark contrast to her pale skin, making her seem like a rare blossom blooming in a forbidden garden.

As Ava beckoned, Ethan fetched her highest heels, his heart pounding with a blend of anticipation and restraint. Kneeling before her, he carefully slipped the heels onto her feet, his touch sending a subtle shiver down her spine. Ava's posture exuded graceful confidence as she extended her leg, their unspoken emotions lingering in the charged silence between them. At that moment, the act of helping her into the heels seemed to symbolize a delicate balance between their past intimacy and the unspoken distance that now loomed large.

As Ava prepares for James to spend the night with her, her request for Ethan's assistance in helping her into her lingerie, and highest heels, and preparing for the evening takes on a deeper significance. Each act of Ethan aiding her dress and preparing for James symbolizes Ava's subtle yet purposeful push for Ethan to embrace his submission to her and, ultimately, to James. Through these seemingly innocent tasks, Ava subtly asserts her dominance and control over Ethan, intertwining their past intimacy with a newfound power dynamic.

As the doorbell rang, Ethan's heart raced with a mixture of apprehension and curiosity. He hesitantly opened the door to James, welcoming him into the living room where Ava awaited, her presence commanding the space with a subtle yet undeniable power. Pouring drinks for the three of them, the clinking of glasses echoed in the room, underscoring the palpable tension that hung in the air.

With each sip, the atmosphere crackled with unspoken desires and silent exchanges. Finally, Ava's voice cut through the charged silence, instructing Ethan to assist James in unrobing. As Ethan approached James, a whirlwind of conflicting emotions swirled within him - a blend of duty, desire, and a deep-seated longing that seemed to pull him inexorably closer to a destiny he couldn't quite grasp.

In this pivotal moment, the intricate dance of power, submission, and unspoken yearning played out, setting the stage for a night that would unravel hidden truths and desires long kept beneath the surface

As she turned to face the mirror, adjusting the straps with delicate movements, Ethan's heart constricted further. The woman he loved was preparing to weave her spell, not for him, but for another. And he, the devoted husband, could only watch as the threads of their marriage continued to unravel.

"Thank you, Ethan," she said, her reflection meeting his in the mirror. There was gratitude in her gaze, yes, but behind it lay a well of complexities and desires that he could neither fulfill nor fathom.

He could only nod, his throat tight, as he faced the bitter truth: the woman he had vowed to cherish was slipping through his fingers, and there was nothing he could do to hold her back.

Ethan paced the length of the living room, each step a measured attempt to calm the storm brewing within him. Shadows lengthened across the floor, mirroring the slow ticking of the clock that counted down the minutes to James' arrival. With each passing second, Ethan's heart grew heavier, the weight of imminent betrayal pressing down on him like an unseen force.

He paused by the window, staring out into the gathering dusk, his reflection a ghostly echo in the glass. The dying light seemed to drain the color from the world, leaving everything washed in shades of gray — a fitting backdrop for the play about to unfold.

In the silence of the house, the whisper of his breath sounded too loud, each inhale sharpened with anticipation, each exhale laced with dread. Ethan closed his eyes briefly, willing himself to find some semblance of control over the emotions churning inside him.

"Control," he muttered under his breath, a bitter laugh escaping his lips. It was a cruel joke, for what control did he have when his wife sought comfort in another's embrace? What power did he wield when his love alone was not enough?

The doorbell shattered the quiet, its chime resonant and final. Ethan's eyes snapped open, a jolt of adrenaline coursing through him. This was it—the moment of truth, the line that once crossed, could never be uncrossed.

He took a deep breath, his chest rising and falling with the effort to steady himself. His hands clenched at his sides, the knuckles whitening as he drew upon every ounce of composure he possessed. He had to be the gracious host, the unsuspecting husband, even while his world crumbled around him.

With steps that felt more mechanical than human, Ethan moved towards the door. He reached out, his hand hovering over the knob for a fraction of a heartbeat before turning it. The door swung open, revealing the figure of James standing on the threshold—a harbinger of change, an agent of pain.

"James, welcome," Ethan managed, his voice steady despite the inner turmoil. A practiced smile found its way onto his face, a mask worn so often it almost felt like a part of him.

"Thank you, Ethan," James replied, stepping inside with a confidence that seemed to fill the space.

As Ethan closed the door behind their guest, sealing the fate of the evening, he couldn't help but feel as though he were also closing the door on a chapter of his life—one that might never be opened again.

Ethan lingered in the periphery, his presence a silent shadow against the stark white walls of the living room. He watched as Ava glided towards James with that same purposeful stride he had come to adore, her emerald eyes shimmering under the soft glow of the chandelier. Their fingers touched in a greeting that seemed too intimate for mere friends, and Ethan's heart clenched.

A laugh escaped Ava's lips, a sound so musical it always had been reserved for moments of genuine delight. But now, it was directed at another man, piercing Ethan's defenses like a finely honed blade. His gaze locked with Ava's for a fleeting moment, the hurt and longing he felt naked within his brown eyes. In hers, a flicker of something unreadable passed—was it guilt? Regret? Or the thrill of newfound attention?

The night wore on, and Ava and James lost in their world of shared jokes and lingering glances. Ethan kept to the edges, fetching drinks and playing the part of the host, all while feeling like an outsider in his own home. With each laugh, each touch, the connection between

Ava and James grew stronger, and more electric, leaving Ethan's skin buzzing with a silent scream for attention.

And finally, Ava led James up the stairs to her bedroom. As James and Ava found themselves in the familiar embrace of the bed she had shared with Ethan for five years, the air between them crackled with tension and unspoken emotions. The transition from the motel to this intimate space tested Ethan's submission to its very limits, each moment laden with the weight of their shared history and diverging paths.

As Ethan stood by, a silent observer of the blossoming connection between Ava and James, a peculiar transformation began within him. Despite the ache of his unrequited love, Ethan couldn't help but feel a surge of intense emotion as he witnessed the genuine happiness that James brought to Ava. In that vulnerable moment, amidst the waves of conflicting emotions, a glimmer of hope sparked within Ethan's heart.

In the soft light filtering through the room, every touch, every glance, carried the weight of years of intimacy and separation. The bed, once a sanctuary of their love, now became a battleground of conflicting desires and unresolved tensions. As Ethan grappled with the resurgence of old feelings and the stark reality of their current dynamic, his submission was pushed to its breaking point.

As James embarked on the intimate journey of undressing Ava, his movements deliberate and unhurried, he savored every moment of revealing her soft, tender skin. With a gentle touch, he traced the path of her dress straps, allowing them to slip down her shoulders, the fabric cascading to the floor like a waterfall of silk. As her bare flesh was unveiled, James's lips became a searing trail of warmth against her delicate skin, igniting a passionate fire that danced along every inch he uncovered.

With a slow, deliberate movement, James lifted his lips to meet hers, a silent promise of desire lingering in the air between them. As their mouths fused in a tender, exploratory kiss, his tongue sought entrance, a dance of passion and longing unfolding with each shared breath. In that intimate moment, as Ava yielded to the caress of his tongue, James's touch found the clasp of her bra, effortlessly releasing it with a deft flick of his thumb and forefinger.

A gasp escaped Ava's lips as her bra fell away, revealing her perfectly sculpted curves to his hungry gaze. The rush of sensation, a blend of anticipation and ecstasy, coursed through her body, echoing in a fervent moan that escaped her lips.

As James tenderly guides Ava to the bed, a silent invitation lingering in his eyes, he turns to Ethan and asks him to come and help him undress. Reluctance tugs at Ethan's heart, a mix of emotions swirling within him as he grapples with the unfolding intimacy before him. Despite his hesitation to fully engage in the moment, when Ava's commanding voice cuts through the air, Ethan finds himself compelled to obey, a sense of duty and longing intertwining in his actions.

As James surrenders to the dominant persona that lay dormant within him, a newfound confidence emanates from his every move, commanding the room with an air of authority that demands attention. With a subtle gesture, he directs his gaze towards the floor, a silent yet unmistakable indication of his expectations for Ethan to kneel before him, a shift in power dynamics palpable in the charged atmosphere.

In a moment thick with tension and unspoken desires, James's silent command hangs in the air, an unyielding force that beckons Ethan to submit to his will. As Ethan hesitantly complies, a wave of anticipation and apprehension washes over him, the weight of James's dominance pressing down on his every action.

As Ethan's conflicting emotions surge within him, a turbulent whirlwind of humiliation and forbidden excitement swirls in his mind, a tumultuous blend of sensations that he struggles to comprehend. The mere notion of aiding his wife's lover in the act of undressing would have been inconceivable mere hours ago, a boundary he never imagined crossing. Yet, in this charged moment, fueled by Ava's commanding presence and the unspoken desires that simmer beneath the surface, an unexpected sense of rightness settles over him, a twisted form of acceptance born from the tangled web of love, duty, and longing.

As Ethan watched Ava and James, a tumult of conflicting emotions washed over him. Helping James undress was a line he never thought he'd cross. The humiliation and excitement warred within him, battling for dominance. How could his loyalty to Ava coexist with this forbidden desire that now seemed so inevitable? Her command felt like a chain, binding him to this twisted dance of submission and longing.

In the hushed atmosphere of the room, Ethan's trembling fingers reached for the intricate laces of James's shoes, each knot a tangible reminder of the surreal situation he found himself in. The weight of his actions bore down on him, a heavy burden he carried as he began to undo the bindings that tethered James to his sense of propriety.

Amidst the delicate dance of untying the shoes, a sound cut through the silence like a shard of glass – Ava's laughter. Its melodic notes hung in the air, a symphony of mystery and mirth that echoed in the corners of Ethan's mind. Was it a mocking melody or a shared secret between them, hidden in plain sight?

As the shoes came off, Ethan carefully placed them aside, each movement deliberate yet laden with unspoken questions. In the wake of this intimate act, James's voice sliced through the tension, a declaration that sent shivers down Ethan's spine. "We will have him properly trained in no time," James proclaimed, his words dripping with implication and intent.

Ava's laughter, like a peal of silver bells, followed James's statement, a crescendo of amusement that reverberated through the room. The sound, louder and more vibrant than before, painted a vivid picture of a shared understanding, a bond that excluded Ethan yet ensnared him in its intricate web.

Humiliation washed over Ethan as he realized that Ava was denigrating him in front of her lover. He knew that he should be incensed by her betrayal but deep down he longed for the humiliation that she was heaping upon him.

In a swift and almost reverent motion, Ethan's hands moved with practiced precision to remove James' socks, a seemingly mundane act laden with unspoken tension. The fabric slipped off James' feet, revealing skin that seemed to hold secrets of its own, a canvas of unspoken desires.

Meanwhile, the room hummed with a silent symphony of intimacy as articles of Ava's clothing cascaded off the bed, a cascade of silk and lace that whispered of hidden vulnerabilities and unspoken truths. The soft thud of fabric meeting plush carpet underscored the charged atmosphere, a delicate dance of revelation and concealment.

As Ethan focused on the task at hand, his fingers deftly worked on James' belt buckle, a tangible barrier holding back a torrent of unspoken desires and forbidden pleasures. The metallic clink of the buckle echoed in the room, a punctuation mark in the unspoken narrative unfolding between the three figures caught in a web of longing and betrayal.

With a sense of inevitability, Ethan's gaze traveled upwards, meeting James' eyes in a silent exchange of understanding and unspoken complicity. As the button on James' trousers yielded under his touch, the fabric pooled at his feet, revealing a truth laid bare in the stark light of desire.

In that moment of revelation, Ethan's eyes were drawn to a sight that stirred conflicting emotions within him – James, unadorned and unapologetically exposed, his arousal a testament to the raw power dynamics at play. Each detail, from the proud angle of James' arousal to the unspoken challenge in his gaze, painted a vivid picture of vulnerability and dominance intertwined in a silent dance of desire.

As Ethan's thoughts flickered between his own body and James', a surge of raw emotion crashed over him, a tumultuous wave of insecurity and desire that threatened to engulf his senses. In that charged moment of comparison, every inch of exposed skin felt like a battlefield, each thought a dagger aimed at his fragile sense of self.

At first glance, the similarities between their bodies offered a fragile sense of solace, a fleeting illusion of parity that crumbled under the weight of his self-doubt. The initial spark of comparison kindled a flame of unease that licked at the edges of his consciousness, whispering insidious doubts and fears that clawed at his resolve.

As James' sinewy figure positioned itself, assertively nestled between Ava's smooth, outstretched legs, Ethan could see his every ripple and contour. His chiseled physique was a constant tormenting reminder of his flaws – fears that gnawed at the edges of his masculine ego. A harsh mirror reflecting what he wished to forget.

James flexed his muscular thighs, grinding down towards Ava with a carnal power that made even Ethan shiver. The honey-tinged skin of his engorged shaft brushed against her inner sanctum, where folds of balmy velvet trembled in anticipation. Glistening beads of arousal coated her delicate petals, highlighting her readiness and desire for him.

Ethan's heart clenched tightly as he watched James begin to explore Ava's sacred garden with tantalizing slowness. Each deliberate thrust was met with a gasp from Ava who clung desperately to the sheets beneath them; eyes closed tight in pleasure.

The room echoed with the squelch of wetness, and the smacking sound of bodies colliding, reverberating like an erotic symphony ringing through each corner - an intimate dance of lustful dominance and delicate surrender, a sight too bitter-sweet for Ethan to bear.

Ethan's gaze was locked onto the rhythmic motion of James' cock disappearing into Ava's slick heat. Her luscious lips parted around him with each slide, taking all he had to offer in this forbidden tryst. The sight was both intoxicating and gut-wrenching for poor Ethan.

Ava herself became Aphrodite incarnate under James' touch. He expertly elicited moans that danced through the air like siren calls made purely for him - sounds accentuated by the sharp hitch in her breath whenever he hit a sweet spot deep within her.

Slowly, rending his gaze away from the spectacle before him, Ethan retreated. Their sounds of ecstasy became a muffled melody in the distance, haunting him as he disappeared into corridors echoing with love and lust that were no longer his to partake in.

In every echo of her pleasure, there resonated a brutal reminder of Ethan's loss – the love he had lost, the desires he could never truly satiate. Ava's gasps of pleasure, James' grunts of satisfaction - these were the sounds that would haunt poor Ethan as he was consumed by a storm of unspoken truths and suppressed desires.

The past and present collided in a whirlwind of emotions, challenging Ethan to navigate the complexities of their relationship with a newfound clarity. How will you capture the raw intensity of this moment as Ethan confronts his deepest fears, desires, and vulnerabilities in the face of Ava's unwavering command?

Then came the shattering moment—the one that would forever be etched into Ethan's soul. It was nothing overt, no grand gesture or explicit declaration. Instead, it was the subtle shift of Ava's body as she leaned into James while they examined a book from the shelf. The way James' hand rested at the small of her back, protective and possessive, a silent claim that screamed louder than words. Ethan watched the scene unfold, his vision tunneling until all he could see was the betrayal of space and touch.

With every fiber of his being screaming to look away, Ethan couldn't tear his gaze from them. It wasn't just the closeness; it was the familiarity, the ease with which they existed in each other's orbit. The intimacy of their encounter was a language he once spoke fluently with Ava, now foreign and forgotten.

As if feeling the weight of Ethan's stare, Ava turned to catch his eye once more. This time, there was no mistaking the message in her gaze—one of sorrow and something deeper, an apology not yet spoken.

Ethan's heart, a fragile vessel of hope and love, fractured under the strain of watching the woman he adored share moments meant for him with another. The pieces scattered, sharp, and jagged, reflecting the light of a marriage that once shone brightly. Now, he stood alone, surrounded by the debris of promises and dreams, wondering if any amount of glue could piece together something so thoroughly broken.

# Chapter Ten - Resolution

Ethan lay in bed, desperate for sleep to take over his weary mind. He closed his eyes and tried to block out the sounds coming from the next room. But every time he felt himself drifting off, a loud thud against the wall reminded him of James's unrelenting pounding on his wife's body. Each impact echoed like a thunderclap, shattering any chance of peaceful slumber.

Ethan clenched his fists in frustration, unable to escape the constant intrusion on his rest. The moans and cries of pleasure mixed with pain assaulted his ears, leaving him unsure if his wife needed help or if she was getting all the "help" she desired.

Finally, blessed silence descended upon the master bedroom. Ethan pulled a pillow over his head, tears streaming down his cheeks as he finally managed to slip into dreamland - though each dream felt more like a haunting nightmare than an escape from reality.

As the sun lazily filtered through the window, Ethan slowly came awake. He lay in bed for a few moments, trying to shake off the lingering feelings of despair and betrayal from the night before. With a heavy heart, he opened the door to the guest bedroom and glanced towards the master bedroom where his wife Ava had spent the night making love to another man.

To his surprise, he heard no sounds coming from the room. No moans of pleasure or creaking of bedsprings. It was as if nothing had happened at all. With a heavy sigh, Ethan made his way down the hall to the bathroom to do his normal morning activities.

He stood in front of the mirror, studying his reflection with tired eyes. The dark circles under his eyes spoke volumes about his sleepless night. He splashed water on his face, hoping it would wash away some of the pain and confusion he was feeling.

As he brushed his teeth, Ethan couldn't help but wonder what James was doing at that moment. Was he still lying in bed with Ava?

Had they already woken up and started their day together? The thought made him sick to his stomach.

With a heavy heart, Ethan finished getting ready for the day. He didn't have any clean clothes, so he slipped on the ones he had worn yesterday and headed towards the kitchen.

He started brewing coffee mechanically, going through familiar motions as he tried to push away thoughts of last night's events. But they kept creeping back into his mind like an unwelcome guest.

As he waited for the coffee to brew, Ethan leaned against the counter and let out a deep sigh. He couldn't believe this was happening to him. This wasn't how marriage was supposed to be. This wasn't how love was supposed to feel.

But despite everything, Ethan still loved Ava with every fiber of his being. And that made all of this even more painful.

As he poured himself a cup of coffee, Ethan decided to try and make breakfast for both of them, hoping that there might be a chance to talk and work through this together. He knew it wouldn't be easy, but he wanted to try.

Ava slowly opened her eyes, the sunlight streaming through the window casting dancing shadows on the walls. Her body felt pleasantly sore from last night's encounter, a reminder of the intensity of her passion with James.

She climbed out of bed, still wrapped in James' embrace, and whispered in his ear, "Ethan's making breakfast, wouldn't you know?"

James couldn't contain his laughter at the thought of

Ava raised an eyebrow at James, knowing full well about his sadistic tendencies. "Please don't torment him any more than necessary," she pleaded.

"But my love, it is necessary to humiliate him. You must decide whether you care more for his feelings or the intense pleasure you feel between those beautiful legs while I ravish you mercilessly." James' words were laced with both admiration and a hint of wickedness. It was a game they played, and Ava knew that deep down, she secretly enjoyed every moment of it.

"Well, then we might as well go down and have some coffee while you figure out what humiliation you want to heap on him next."

As Ethan reluctantly served breakfast to Ava and James, his hands trembled slightly, betraying the turmoil within him. James' commanding presence at the table seemed to fill the room, casting a shadow over Ethan's meek attempts at normalcy. The clatter of dishes seemed louder, more grating, as Ethan placed a plate delicately in front of James, his movements almost mechanical. Despite the ache in his heart, he poured coffee into two mugs, the bitter aroma mingling with the tension that hung heavy in the air.

Ethan excused himself and left the room, going up to get some fresh clothes to wear for the day. He heard both his wife and her lover laughing as he started up the stairs. He knew that he was the brunt of the joke and he vowed to have a hard conversation with Ava once James left. As he pulled on the last of his clothes and did up the buttons he heard the front door open and close and he hoped that it was James leaving.

When he once again entered the kitchen, he saw his wife standing staring out of the window.

Ethan's restraint shattered, the dam of his silence breaking under the torrent of emotions he could no longer contain. He surged forward, the muscles in his jaw clenching as he grasped Ava's shoulders, forcing her to face him.

"Ava, how could you?" His voice was a ragged blade, cutting through the pretense and the delicate balance they had both maintained for so long. "How can you stand there with him, touching, laughing, sharing what was ours?"

Ava's eyes, those deep pools of emerald, widened, her lips parting in shock. But it wasn't just surprise that flashed across her features; it was the dawning understanding of the pain she had inflicted, the cost of her desires etched into the lines of Ethan's face.

"Please, Ethan... I..." Her words faltered, choked by the realization that the chasm between them had been her own doing.

"Tell me," he pressed on, his hands trembling as they slid from her shoulders, the anger giving way to raw agony. "Tell me why my love wasn't enough. Why the passion we shared has grown so cold in your heart that you had to seek warmth in another's embrace?"

Tears breached Ava's defenses, spilling over the rims of her eyelids, and trailing down her cheeks like liquid sorrow. She reached out, her fingertips barely brushing against Ethan's forearm, seeking solace or forgiveness, or perhaps both.

"Your love has always been enough," she whispered, her voice heavy with the weight of their fractured fairy tale. "But love and lust are two different things. I am in love with you but you don't satisfy me sexually. James is everything in bed that you are not. Ethan. While making you happy, I forgot about what I needed, and when I met James again, I knew what I was missing."

"James offered you an escape," Ethan finished for her, the hurt in his eyes now mingled with comprehension. He had always known Ava was a tempest of complexities, a woman who danced on the edge of fulfillment and yearning. He had tried to be her anchor, but in doing so, perhaps he had only tethered her spirit too tightly.

"More than an escape," Ava admitted, the confession hanging between them, an acknowledgment of her betrayal but also her inner turmoil.

They stood there, husband and wife, at the precipice of all they had built, their voices spent from shouting, now only breathing the same air thick with anguish and longing. The echoes of their argument resonated through the once-happy home, a testament to the love that still smoldered beneath the ash of their discord.

As Ava's tears continued to fall, they were a silent plea, a bridge over the chasm that gaped wide and menacing. And Ethan, with his kind brown eyes clouded by grief, knew that the choice before them was not just about forgiveness, but whether the love they shared could evolve beyond the pain they had endured.

Ava's trembling fingers wiped the remnants of tears from her cheeks, the weight of her husband's anguish still palpable in the air. She turned away from Ethan's pained figure, his body hunched like a tree after a storm, and walked toward the window, her gaze lost to the night sky.

Her heart beat with an irregular rhythm, echoing the turmoil that churned within. Ava knew she stood at the threshold of a decision, one that carried with it the gravity of altering their lives forever. The reflection staring back at her from the dark glass was a woman caught in the throes of desire and loyalty, each battling for supremacy.

She let her fingertips graze the cool surface of the pane, tracing patterns as if they could map out the solution to her dilemma. Behind her, the house remained silent, save for the occasional creak of wood – a testament to the tension that held its breath within these walls.

As she stood there, the memory of James' touch lingered on her skin, a ghostly sensation that promised both ecstasy and devastation. It was the same sensation that had beckoned her to cross lines she once believed unassailable, leading her to this precipice where the future awaited her command.

Closing her eyes, Ava inhaled deeply, searching for clarity amidst the chaos of her emotions. She sought the measured calm that always guided her, but it felt just beyond her grasp, replaced by the tempest of her own needs.

Finally, with the day as her witness, Ava turned from the window, her resolve slowly knitting together. She faced the hall that led back to Ethan, to the life they had shared, every step an echo of the vows they had exchanged. Her love for him was undeniable, but so too was the hunger for something more, something that had found its shape in the form of another man.

"Can love be enough?" she whispered into the silence, her voice a blend of hope and despair.

With a quiet determination, Ava knew what she had to do. The choice lay before her, stark and immutable. It was time to decide whether to cling to the comfort of the familiar or to brave the uncertainty of change.

Tonight, her decision would mark the end of one chapter and the beginning of another. It would be the stroke of the pen that wrote the future of her marriage and the map of her happiness. And so, Ava Myers, a silhouette against the moonlight, took a breath and stepped forward, her path irrevocably chosen.

# Chapter Eleven – Total Submission

Ava sank into the plush depths of their living room sofa, the familiar comfort offering little solace to the tempest brewing inside her. The thrumming of her heart kept a relentless pace, each beat a hammer against her ribs as she steeled herself for the conversation that could unravel the tapestry of their five-year union. Ethan, with his ever-present warm smile that softened the edges of life's harsher moments, settled beside her, unaware of the impending storm.

"Sweetheart?" His voice, a gentle caress, laced with concern as he searched her face, those kind brown eyes trying to decipher the silent language of her troubled expression.

Ava inhaled deeply, the air filling her lungs like a buoyant force, lifting her resolve. She turned to face him, her emerald eyes locking onto his with an intensity that was both a plea and a declaration. For years, she had cloaked her dissatisfaction, draped it behind the veils of smiles and subtle nods, but the façade was wearing thin, threadbare, and translucent.

"Ethan," she began, her voice a steady stream flowing over pebbles of trepidation, "I love you. There's no corner of my heart where you aren't etched deep and permanent." Her words, sincere and heavy with truth, hung between them, a fragile bridge over a chasm of unsaid things.

She paused, her fingers tracing the soft fabric of the couch, gathering strength from the threads woven tight and strong. "But there's something I can't ignore any longer," Ava continued, her voice thick with emotion. The confession percolated on her tongue, bittersweet and daunting. "It's about us, about me... I need more, Ethan. The kind of fulfillment, the passion, that I've found with James."

The silence that followed was deafening, a vacuum that seemed to suck all the air from the room. Her declaration stood stark and bold between them, a naked truth that refused to be dressed in excuses or half-truths any longer. Ava watched the myriad of emotions play across Ethan's features—love battling with hurt, comprehension grappling with disbelief. She reached out tentatively, seeking his hand, a lifeline for them both in the swirling uncertainty of her admission.

Ethan's countenance transformed, a silent play of emotions that Ava read like the familiar pages of their shared history. Shock etched deep lines around his mouth; hurt flickered in the downturn of his lips; confusion danced in the furrows of his brow. She could almost hear the cogs of his mind grinding against this new, unwelcome knowledge, trying to mesh it into the reality they had built together.

Extending her hand, her fingers brushed against his, a whisper of contact that sought to ground him amidst the chaos. The warmth of his skin was a balm, a silent promise that she was there with him, even as she stood at the precipice of this seismic shift in their marriage.

"Listen to me, Ethan," Ava said, her voice a lifeline thrown across the widening gap between them. "I've been turning this over in my mind, night after night, feeling every contour of our love and where it falls short." Her hand squeezed his, a pulse of connection that tethered them to this moment. "I can't keep pretending that my desires don't exist, or that they can be fulfilled within the walls of what we have always known."

The words spilled from her, each syllable heavy with the weight of countless sleepless nights spent wrestling with her longing for something more, something elemental that she found in her fiery encounters with James. She watched Ethan's face, observed the subtle shift as he absorbed her confession, the slow nod that didn't signify agreement but an understanding of the depth of her turmoil.

"James brings out a passion in me that I can't just switch off," she continued, her voice threading through the air between them, binding her truth to his heart. "It's not a reflection on you or the love I have for you. It's about acknowledging a part of myself that I've tried to bury for the sake of us. But I can't do that anymore, not without losing a part of who I am."

Her revelation hung in the space, a raw and vulnerable truth that asked for acceptance in its most unadorned form. Ava held Ethan's gaze, her emerald eyes pools of earnest yearning, seeking not just his forgiveness but his understanding.

Ethan's breath caught a single tear betraying the calm exterior he so desperately clung to. It traced a path down his cheek, an eloquent testament to the turmoil within. Ava's heart contracted at the sight, her own eyes stinging with empathy for the man she loved in ways beyond measure.

"I understand if you can't accept this," Ava said, her voice a gentle caress meant to soothe the sting of her revelation. "But I can't starve myself of the sexual fulfillment that's become as vital to me as breathing." Her words were a whispered confession of her deepest needs, an intimate admission shared in the sacred space of their shared life.

Ethan sat motionless, his hand still enveloped by hers, the warmth between their fingers a stark contrast to the cold dread that seemed to settle in his chest. He looked down at their entwined hands, a symbol of the connection they'd built over years, now threatened by an invisible wedge.

Ava watched him, her breath held captive by the moment. She could see the battle behind his eyes, the struggle to reconcile his love for her with the piercing truth of her desires. Pain etched lines across his forehead, but there was a resolute set to his jaw, a silent promise that he wouldn't give up on them without a fight.

Moments passed, each one laden with the gravity of her confession, stretching out like the quiet before a storm. Ethan's silence spoke volumes, and in it, Ava heard all the words he couldn't bring himself to say. She gave him time, time to navigate the labyrinth of emotions her plea had unleashed.

In the stillness of their living room, where memories of laughter and tenderness painted the walls, they sat together—two hearts bound by love, yet pulled taut by unspoken fears and unmet needs.

Ethan inhaled sharply, breaking the silence that had settled over them like a thick fog. He raised his gaze from their hands, now untangling his fingers from Ava's to wipe away the moisture that lingered at the edge of his eyes. His voice, when he spoke, trembled with the weight of acceptance—a man conceding to a battle he never anticipated fighting.

"Look at me, Ava," he said, his brown eyes pools of sorrow and love. "I can't... I can't stand the thought of losing you. If this is what you need—if James is what you need—I won't be the one to hold you back." The words seemed to cost him, each one etched with the pain of surrender.

Ava felt the shift in the air, the bittersweet taste of victory mingled with the sting of betrayal. Her heart expanded with an overwhelming rush of gratitude, her breath catching in her throat as she reached out, her hand trembling slightly as she cupped Ethan's cheek, feeling the warmth of his skin against her palm.

"Thank you," she whispered, her eyes searching his for any sign of resentment. Finding none, only the immense depth of his affection for her, she continued, "I promise you, Ethan, I will be honest with you about everything. About James.

The gravity of her words hung between them, a solemn vow spoken amidst the turmoil of their shared predicament. At that moment, Ava knew the measure of the man before her; a man whose love was so vast, that it could encompass even the parts of her that reached beyond their union, into the arms of another.

Ethan's arm tentatively reached out, his fingers brushing against Ava's. With a gentle tug, he drew her closer until she was enveloped in his embrace. His chest rose and fell unevenly against her cheek, the rhythm of a heart grappling with tumultuous emotions. Ava nestled into him, her body molding to his as if they were two pieces of a puzzle that, despite everything, still fit perfectly together.

In the sanctuary of Ethan's arms, Ava found refuge from the storm of her own making. Her pulse, which had been racing with anxiety and fear, began to slow, syncing with the steady beat against her ear. They remained locked in silence, their shared understanding transcending the need for words, each breath they took knitting together the frayed edges of their bond.

As the initial shock of their conversation faded into the background, Ava realized they were on the precipice of a new chapter. Time stretched out before them, a canvas upon which their fears and dreams could be laid bare.

"Talk to me, Ava," Ethan murmured, his voice a low rumble that seemed to reverberate through her very being. "Tell me what you're thinking."

And so she did. Ava spoke of the restlessness that coursed through her veins, a yearning for passion that had gone unfulfilled within the confines of their marriage bed. She spoke of James—of the fire he ignited within her—but always circled back to the love that anchored her to Ethan.

Ethan shared his fears, his voice a soft confession in the dim light of their living room. He feared losing her, the distance that might grow between them, and the uncertainty that now hung over their future. But he also spoke of hope—the hope that their love could weather this storm, evolve, and adapt in ways they had never anticipated.

They delved into dreams too, ones that still shimmered with potential. A small cottage by the ocean that Ava had always fancied, the laughter of children they both desired to one day echo through the halls of their home, the travels they had outlined on back-of-napkin itineraries during late-night conversations.

As the hours slipped by, Ava and Ethan wove a tapestry of vulnerability and strength, their voices intertwining to create a narrative of resilience. Together, they painted a picture not just of acceptance, but of a love complex and robust enough to embrace even the most unconventional threads of their lives.

Ava stirred, the soft light of morning filtering through the sheer curtains and casting a warm glow across the room. She blinked the remnants of sleep away and turned, her gaze landing on Ethan who sat propped against the headboard, watching her. His eyes were pools of affection mingled with an echo of yesterday's hurt, yet there was a resolve in them, a silent vow that spoke volumes.

"Good morning," she whispered, reaching out to trace the line of his jaw with the back of her fingers. He caught her hand, pressing a kiss to her palm, the tenderness in the gesture weaving a comforting thread through the complexity of their situation.

"Morning," he replied, his voice low and rough with emotion. They lay there for a moment, the air between them thick with words unspoken, each breath a shared acknowledgment of the path they had chosen to embark upon.

Ava shifted closer, resting her head against his chest, listening to the steady rhythm of his heart. It was a sound that promised constancy amidst the tumult of change, a reminder that despite the passions that pulled her elsewhere, the core of her world remained steadfast in Ethan's embrace.

"Are we okay?" she murmured against his skin, the question laden with the weight of their decisions.

Ethan wrapped an arm around her, his hold firm and reassuring. "We're more than okay," he said. "We have love, Ava. That's our foundation. We'll figure the rest out, together."

In the quiet embrace of the dawn, as they lay entwined, the dappled sunlight painted a serene scene over them, casting shadows that couldn't hide the turbulence brewing within Ethan. Despite the calm exterior, a storm of emotions raged inside him. As his desire for Ava pulsed through him, he reached out, seeking solace in her touch, only to be met with a cold reality. When Ava sensed his intentions, she recoiled her rejection a sharp reminder of the barriers between them. "That isn't part of the deal," her words pierced through the tranquility, slicing through Ethan's heart. The conflict between his longing for her and her unwavering loyalty to James created a chasm that seemed impossible to bridge.

Ava traced the rim of her wine glass, a crimson drop clinging to the edge like a secret waiting to spill over. The candlelight flickered across the table, casting a warm glow on Ethan's face as they sat in their refurbished dining room—a space that once felt mundane now charged with an air of anticipation.

"Remember when we first moved in?" Ethan asked, his eyes reflecting the flame's dance. "We were so sure about everything."

Ava nodded, her emerald eyes meeting his. They had repainted these walls together, argued over furniture, and laughed through every unexpected leak and creak. "Certainty has its charms, but uncertainty... it has its allure," she said, her voice threaded with a newfound edge of daring.

Ethan reached across the table, his fingers brushing hers, a silent vow renewing with each touch. They had embarked on a journey neither had anticipated, exploring desires that pushed them beyond the boundaries they once held sacred. It was a delicate dance of love and longing, each step taking them further into the depths of their unconventional union.

It was on a night like any other, yet unlike any before, that Ava stood entwined with James, her back arched against his chest, his hands tracing the contours of her body with an artist's precision. The air was heavy with desire as Ethan watched from the doorway, his presence a silent testament to the trust and understanding that now defined their marriage.

The sight of Ava, head thrown back in ecstasy, her raven hair cascading like a waterfall of midnight silk, struck a chord deep within

Ethan. There was a beauty in her surrender, a poetry in the way James's hands claimed her with a passion that mirrored her hunger. And yet, beneath the layers of lust and pleasure, Ethan saw the unshakeable core of their love, a flame that burned steadily amidst the whirlwind of their desires.

As Ava's breath hitched, her gaze caught Ethan's, a silent exchange passing between them. In that lingering look was every promise made and kept, every fear acknowledged and assuaged. Together, they were rewriting the rules of their world, not with reckless abandon, but with a reverence for the love that held them steadfast.

And as the chapter drew to a close, Ava in James's passionate embrace, Ethan knew that their story was far from over. It was simply evolving, transforming into a tale of boundless love, one that they would continue to write with each beat of their brave, unyielding hearts.

# Chapter Twelve – Ava's Happily Ever After

The sun had long set, casting the living room in a soft glow from the dimmed lights. Ava led Ethan to their plush sofa, her every move deliberate and assured. They sat down together, their bodies close but not touching, a mirror of the emotional gap that had been widening between them. Her fingers reached for his, entwining with a gentle firmness that belied the gravity of their conversation.

"Thank you, Ethan," she began, her voice steady and infused with a deep sincerity. "Thank you for being open to this... to us finding a new way forward." The emerald pools of her eyes locked with his, an unspoken plea for understanding shimmering within their depths.

Ethan, with a warm smile that masked the turmoil behind his kind brown eyes, nodded. His heart raced, a mix of fear and love churning in his chest. He knew the significance of this moment, the precipice upon which their marriage teetered.

Ava inhaled slowly, gathering her thoughts like an artist who selects colors for a canvas. "I need to take control, Ethan," she confessed, her words painting a picture of longing and unfulfilled desires. "I need to embrace my sexual needs fully, without restraint or hesitation."

He watched her, her grace palpable even in stillness, waiting for the pieces of the puzzle she laid before him to form a complete image.

"It's not a punishment," she continued, her hand squeezing his in reassurance. "It's liberation. For both of us." Ava exhaled, a breath she'd been holding for years. "I want you to become my willing servant. To manage our home—the cooking, the cleaning, the laundry—so that I can truly explore what I desire."

Ethan's heart skipped a beat. His role would change, from partner to supporter in a play where he wasn't sure of his lines. Yet, as he looked into Ava's pleading eyes, he understood that this was about more than chores; it was about salvaging the remnant embers of their union.

"Can you do this for me? For us?" Ava's voice was almost a whisper, yet it echoed loudly in the silence that enveloped them.

Ethan's mind reeled with the implications, but his love for Ava anchored him. He squeezed her hand back, a silent vow to traverse this uncertain path by her side.

Ethan sat motionless, his fingers interlaced with Ava's as he absorbed the gravity of her proposition. The air between them hummed with silent tension, a stark contrast to the rhythmic ticking of the grandfather clock in the corner. He searched her face, seeking reassurance in her emerald gaze, which held him with an intensity that was both unnerving and electrifying.

"James," Ava began, her voice steady, "I want him to stay in the Master Bedroom. Full-time." Her declaration hung heavily in the room, each word weighted with implication.

Ethan's heart thudded against his ribcage, threatening to betray the calm facade he fought to maintain. He knew James, after all, the man who held a mirror to the desires Ava harbored, desires that Ethan had struggled to fulfill.

"It's not... It's not about us failing," Ava continued, her hand giving him a gentle squeeze, grounding him. "It's about redefining our connection, strengthening it differently."

With each breath, Ethan felt the familiar contours of their life together shift into something new, something unknown. Yet the unwavering resolve in Ava's posture, the purposeful tilt of her chin, spoke volumes of her commitment to this path. And it was in that moment, watching her outline the future with careful precision, that Ethan understood the depth of his devotion.

"Okay," he whispered, the word scarcely audible. The apprehension mingled with a fierce desire to see Ava fulfilled, to see her step into the fullness of her being—even if it meant reshaping his role into that of a spectator, a facilitator.

"Thank you," Ava breathed out, her relief palpable. She leaned forward, planting a soft kiss on his forehead, a benediction for the journey ahead. They were crossing a threshold, together yet apart, bound by a love that demanded sacrifice and courage in equal measure.

As they stood, hands still joined, the last vestiges of daylight fading from the living room, Ethan stepped into his new reality, one where his willingness to serve would become the cornerstone of their evolving marriage.

Ethan's fingers hovered over the brass handle of his suitcase, a vessel for more than just clothes—it was to be the carrier of a life he had known and now was leaving behind. He unzipped it with a slow, deliberate motion, folding his shirts with care, their fabric whispering as each layer met the next. The scent of lavender from Ava's sachets clung to the cotton, a reminder of their shared space, of nights entwined in these very threads.

"Are you alright?" Ava's voice, soft yet certain, cut through the stillness of the room.

He looked up, meeting her emerald gaze, finding resolve where uncertainty once swam. "I am," Ethan replied, the truth of his words surprising even himself. "It's... different, but I'm here for you, Ava. For us." His devotion lay bare in that admission, a sacrifice on the altar of their love.

Ava nodded, her hands smoothing over the stack of linens she cradled against her chest. She moved with grace, every step a measured dance as she transported parts of their shared life across the threshold of the master bedroom. The one she would now occupy with James.

The guest bedroom felt smaller, the walls closing in with a sense of permanence as Ethan settled his belongings into the dresser. Each drawer slid open with a creak, a chorus of new beginnings, or perhaps, silent eulogies for what was being left behind.

Their movements around the house took on a ritualistic quality, a silent ballet choreographed by necessity and the will to redefine. The tension hung heavy—a tapestry woven with threads of anticipation for the uncharted territories of their hearts.

"Need help with that?" Ethan offered as he noticed Ava balancing a box labeled 'Memories' with an unwieldy bulkiness.

"Please." Her smile didn't quite reach her eyes, but there was gratitude there, a shared understanding as he relieved her of the weight.

Together they shuffled the contents of their lives into their new respective spaces, the division of two worlds under one roof. Ethan could feel the change, a tangible shift as the essence of their marriage adapted to the contours of this new arrangement.

As evening drew near, and shadows played upon the walls, Ethan found himself standing at the threshold of the guest room, a world apart from where he had begun the day. The air was thick with the unknown, but within it, he sensed the promise of transformation, for Ava, for himself, for the love that was brave enough to venture into the depths of desire.

The hush of twilight settled over the master bedroom as Ava lingered by the window, her silhouette framed against the fading light. Ethan watched her from the doorway, every line and curve of her body etched into his memory like a cherished sonnet.

"Beautiful sunset," she murmured, not turning to face him but knowing he was there—as always.

"Yeah," he echoed softly, taking tentative steps into the room that had cradled their love for years. A sanctuary now transformed into a stage for their next act.

He approached her, wrapping his arms around her waist from behind, resting his chin on her shoulder. The scent of her hair was intoxicating, familiar yet tinged with the unknown.

"Remember when we painted these walls?" Ava's voice cracked slightly, betraying her composure.

Ethan smiled against her skin. "I got more paint on me than the wall."

They both chuckled, a fleeting moment of levity in the gravity of the hour. Yet, beneath the laughter, there lingered a sadness—a mourning for the simplicity they were leaving behind.

Ava turned within his embrace, facing him, her emerald eyes locking onto his. "Ethan," she began, her tone resolute, "there's something I need you to do for me—for us."

"Anything," he whispered, though a tremor of uncertainty quivered through him.

In the throes of anticipation, Ava's eyes remained locked onto Ethan's, a silent challenge that he accepted willingly. He guided James, the granite-like hardness of him tingling against his fingertips, to the dewy petals of her femininity. The intimacy was amplified by the mere inches that separated them, and the sexually charged moment strummed through him like an electrifying chord.

"Take it slow," Ava instructed, releasing a breathy moan as James entered her with a calculated slowness. She gasped at his intrusion, her velvety folds enveloping him greedily.

Their rhythm started slowly, a sensual dance that had Ethan captivated. His heart pounded in his chest as he watched James piston into Ava, his body fully engrossed in the act. The heavy slap of flesh on flesh echoed around them - a carnal chorus that served as an unspeakable testament to their shared desire.

Ethan took himself in hand, unable to resist the call of his arousal. He stroked himself in time with each thrust, each retreat, waves of intense need cascading over him as he watched James bury himself inside Ava again and again.

Her cries were the kind you read about yet never truly understand until you hear them - they were primal and raw and filled with yearning. They fueled Ethan further; propelling him down this path of submission and leaving him intoxicated with the heady mixture of guilt and pleasure. Her nails dug into James' back as if she were anchoring herself against the storm she'd summoned.

The room was filled with an animalistic symphony of grunts, sighs, and erotic whispers that promised debauchery beyond reason. Sweat trickled down their bodies - droplets shining like liquid diamonds against their feverish skin.

She commanded Ethan to kneel closer, bringing him right up to where their bodies joined in sinful unity. Close enough to feel the damp heat, to smell her musky scent mingled with James' masculine one.

"Watch," she said, her eyes glazed over in lusty abandonment.

Ethan watched and felt himself harden further at the sight of James sliding in and out of Ava's silky chute. He took note of each ecstatic whimper that slipped from her lips, each guttural growl that rumbled from James' throat.

His own hands found their way back to his arousal, stroking in rhythm with their movements. His groans added a bass note to their symphony of pleasure as he neared his climax, mirroring theirs.

As Ava trembled beneath James, her finish washed over him too, leaving him drained and panting. Ethan kept his eyes on them as Ava's body quivered from aftershocks while James spilled his seed inside Ava - marking her internally in a way only he could.

Ethan pressed his palm against his own spent length, shivering upon feeling the coolness of his release smeared on his fingers. His gaze was drawn back to Ava who lay flushed and sprawled on the bed; radiating satisfaction. She beckoned him closer with a crooked finger, whispering instructions that would lead him further into unknown territory.

When the time came for Ethan to fulfill his promise and clean them up with careful laps of his tongue, he did so without flinching. The taste was shocking at first but not entirely unpleasant - an erotic cocktail of all three participants' flavors served fresh after sensuous lovemaking.

Their bodies were still intertwined when Ethan finished, casting them all into a silence filled with soft pants and gentle caresses. It was an unexpected turn of events filled with shocking displays of submission, possession, and surrender - Yet it was unquestionably the most profound show of trust Ethan had ever witnessed.

The soft rustle of sheets whispered through the stillness of the night as Ava turned in her bed, the silken fabric caressing her skin with every subtle movement. The moonlight cast a gentle glow across the room, illuminating her solitary form nestled within the expanse of the master bedroom. Her emerald eyes, usually so full of fiery determination, now fluttered closed, heavy with the exhaustion that comes from indulging in long-suppressed desires.

Across the hallway, in the smaller confines of the guest room, Ethan lay rigid on his back, staring at the ceiling with a gaze that penetrated the mundane plaster. His mind was adrift in the sea of change that had flooded their lives, his thoughts an intricate dance between concern and arousal. Though his body yearned for rest, there was a palpable tension that held him captive to wakefulness—an echo of the passion he had witnessed and the new role he had willingly accepted.

Ava's voice, reduced to a mere whisper in the shadowed chamber, reached out to James, who remained by her side, his presence a testament to the transformation that had seized control of their lives. "Thank you," she murmured, the words infused with an intimacy that transcended the physical realm. "For understanding me... for embracing this with me."

James, his silhouette outlined by the dim light, leaned closer, his breath hot upon her ear as he reciprocated with a vow wrapped in velvet darkness. "I am yours, Ava. In every way you desire," he assured, his tone laced with a promise of severity that belied the tenderness of the moment. "And I will be the guardian of your pleasures, ensuring that Ethan knows his place and purpose."

A frisson of excitement sparked within Ava at his words, igniting a flame that threatened to consume all doubts. She could feel the power of their connection, the strength of their bond solidifying with each shared secret and uttered vow. It was then that a thought, bold and intoxicating, took shape in her mind. "Perhaps it's time we set firm rules for Ethan," she suggested, her voice steady despite the racing of her heart. "If he falters in his duties..."

"Then he shall be disciplined," James finished for her, his voice a low growl that resonated with authority. "He must learn that his servitude is not a choice but a commitment to our happiness."

A sense of fulfillment enveloped Ava as she considered the path they were embarking upon. There was no room for hesitation, no space for second-guessing. They had crossed into uncharted territory, and there was only forward momentum now. And as the night yielded to the encroaching dawn, Ava found solace in the complexity of their entwined lives, each participant locked in a dance of dominance, submission, and the relentless pursuit of pleasure.

The gentle rise and fall of James's chest beneath Ava's cheek lulled her towards the edge of sleep, a rhythmic comfort that whispered promises of safety and devotion. Her arm draped over him possessively, the warmth of his skin seeping into hers, branding her with an invisible mark of ownership. His heartbeat was a steady drum, a soothing melody to the chaotic symphony that had played out earlier in the night.

Ava's mind, though weary, danced with vivid images of the evening's events—the look of resigned surrender in Ethan's eyes, the feel of James's powerful hands guiding her body to new heights, the sound of her voice as she commanded and dictated the terms of their twisted love triangle. With each recollection, a thrill surged through her, fierce and unapologetic.

She shifted slightly, pressing closer to James, savoring the contact of their entwined limbs. The realization crept into her consciousness, unfurling like the petals of a dark bloom. She would cross any boundary, and break any taboo, if it meant preserving the ecstasy that James could evoke within her. Ethan's role in this hedonistic play was clear—he was the pawn, the instrument through which she could exercise her control and satiate her burgeoning desires.

The thought should have jarred her and sent tremors of guilt through her heart, but it didn't. Instead, it anchored her, grounded her in the knowledge that she had power here, power that was intoxicating and absolute. Ava's lips curved in a sleepy smile against James's skin, her breath a whisper of contentment against his pulse.

"Anything for you," she murmured, words lost in the sanctuary of their shared silence. "Anything."

James's hand found hers under the covers, fingers twining with a possessive strength that spoke volumes. It was an affirmation, a silent vow that echoed her readiness to venture further down this path.

Ethan's face flickered behind her eyelids, a specter of a life they once knew—a life that now felt distant, a mere shadow cast by the brilliant blaze of her newfound purpose. A pang of something akin to compassion flickered within her, but it was quickly smothered by the overwhelming desire to please James, to be his queen in a kingdom where pleasure ruled supreme and Ethan served at their feet.

As sleep claimed her, drawing her into its embrace with the allure of dreams yet to be woven, Ava surrendered to the night, to the tangled bodies and souls that sought refuge in the oblivion of slumber. And in that moment of vulnerability, her last conscious thought was a pledge, a sacred oath to the man who had awakened her true nature.

"Everything I am, everything I will be—it's yours, James. Even if it means debasing Ethan."

The End

# Don't miss out!

Visit the website below and you can sign up to receive emails whenever Wanda Peters publishes a new book. There's no charge and no obligation.

https://books2read.com/r/B-A-COFL-SKPAD

**BOOKS 2 READ**

Connecting independent readers to independent writers.

Did you love *An Old Flame For Ava*? Then you should read *Cracks in the Vow Six Stories of Love's Demise*[1] by Wanda Peters!

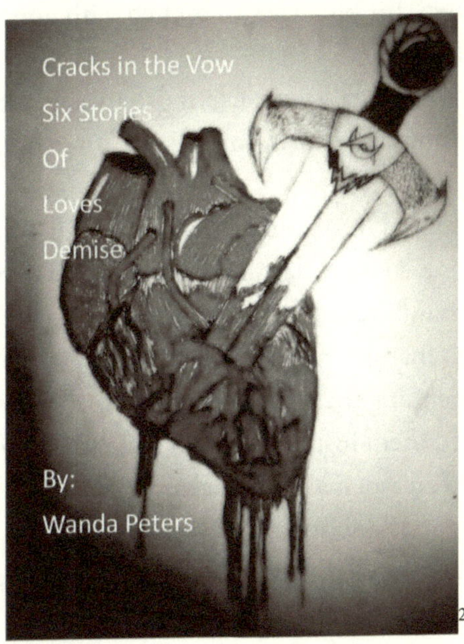


Fairy tails always in with the words, "and they lived happily ever after". Unfortunately, real life is not a fairy tale.

Roger Strong stood in front of the large, ornate doors of his mansion, his arms outstretched as if welcoming the world. He took a deep breath, the crisp autumn air filling his lungs with a sense of satisfaction. Everything was falling into place, just as he had planned.

He turned to face his newest guests, a young couple in their early twenties. The bride, a delicate beauty with long blonde hair and sparkling blue eyes, clung to her fiancé's arm, her excitement palpable.

"Welcome to my home, my dear friends," Roger said, his voice smooth and inviting. "I am so pleased to have you here."

---

1. https://books2read.com/u/3nq808

2. https://books2read.com/u/3nq808

The groom, a tall and handsome man with a confident stride, smiled at Roger. "Thank you for having us, Mr. Strong. Your reputation precedes you."

Roger chuckled, his blue eyes twinkling with amusement. "Please, call me Roger. I insist."

The bride blushed, her gaze flickering between Roger and her new husband "It's an honor to meet you, Roger. Your home is absolutely stunning."

Roger's lips curved into a smile, his charm radiating from him like a warm sun. "Thank you, my dear. I take great pride in my home. And I assure you, your stay here will be nothing short of perfection."

The couple exchanged a look of awe, their excitement growing at the thought of spending their honeymoon in such a luxurious setting.

Roger ushered them inside, his hand lightly resting on the small of the bride's back. "Please, make yourselves at home. The staff will take care of your luggage and show you to your rooms."

As the couple marveled at their surroundings, Roger made his way to the grand staircase, his mind buzzing with anticipation. He couldn't believe his luck. Everything had fallen into place so perfectly as if fate itself was on his side.

He had been planning this for years, patiently biding his time until the right opportunity presented itself. And when he heard about this young couple, their impending wedding, and their dream of a luxurious honeymoon, he knew it was the perfect opportunity to put his plan into action.

Roger had always been drawn to young, innocent women. There was something about their naivety and vulnerability that fueled his desires. And he had found a way to fulfill those desires without any consequences.

He had built his fortune on the promise of extravagant vacations to young couples, offering them the perfect escape from their mundane lives. What they didn't know was that his true intention was to seduce the bride before the consummation of her marriage.

This is the beginning of just one story of love lost

# Also by Wanda Peters

10 Reasons You Should Cuckold Your Husband
Cruel Wife, Slave Husband
Embracing My Inner Bitch
Erotic Short Stories of Dominance and Submission
Cuckolded By A Stranger, An Erotic Novel
Cuckolded By His Boss
The Hot Wife Club
Cuckolded and Bound for Punishment
Cuckolded By My Best Friend
Cuckold's Anonymous
An Anniversary To Remember
My Wife's Surprise
Training Her Cuckold Husband
A Little Devil in Georgia
His Mother's Advice
Addicted To High Heels or A Slave To My Wife's Boots
The Huntress
A Wedding to Remember
Evil Under a Western Sky
Cuckolding The Bootlicker
Bondage and Discipline 101
Tales of Love, Romance and Marriage
The Evil Therapist Returns
Cracks in the Vow Six Stories of Love's Demise
Two Books Of Domination And Legal Thrillers

# An Old Flame For Ava

# About the Author

I have been writing erotica for the past 15 years. Most of what I write is about dominant wives and submissive husbands. Occasionally I will write a book about a submissive woman because that seems to be what some readers want.

9 798224 039364